致敬译界巨匠许渊冲先生

许渊冲译
李商隐诗选

SELECTED POEMS OF LI SHANGYIN

编译

许渊冲

中国出版集团
中译出版社

目录 Contents

译序

李商隐也许是全世界第一个象征派朦胧诗人，比法国19世纪的朦胧诗人马拉美早了1000多年。要把我国诗词译成英文很不容易，要把李商隐的朦胧诗译成英文更是难上加难。因为中文是一种文学的语言，英文却是一种科学的语言。科学要求精确，说一是一，说二是二，言尽意穷；文学却要丰富，要能说一指二，一中见多，意在言外。

我国的诗词更是如此，而李商隐的无题诗可以说是典型。

我们先来看看李商隐最著名的无题诗："相见时难别亦难，东风无力百花残。春蚕到死丝方尽，蜡炬成灰泪始干。晓镜但愁云鬓改，夜吟应觉月光寒。蓬山此去无多路，青鸟殷勤为探看。"第一句两个"难"字，一个是"难得"的意思，一个是"难过"的意思，同一个字包含两种不同的内容，因此可以说字的内容大于形式。第二句据周汝昌说，"东风无力"是"百花残"的原因，但诗句中并没有因果关系的字样，这又说明诗的形式小于诗的内容。第三句的"丝"字既指蚕丝，又暗指"相思"，第四句的"泪"字既指蜡泪，又指情人的眼泪，也是一语双关。第五、第六句没有主语，译者既可理解为诗人“夜吟”，也可理解为女方对“镜”发“愁”，而这正是朦胧诗的妙处。但英语是一种精确的语言，一般说来，句中不能没有主语。因此，一定要指明发愁的是诗人还是女方。英译文能不能表达原诗的朦胧美呢？下面，我们先来看看英国译者 A. C. Graham 在《晚唐诗选》中的译文：

For ever hard to meet, and as hard to part.
Each flower spoils in the failing east wind;
Spring's silkworms wind till death their heart's threads;
The wick of the candle turns to ash before its tears dry.
Morning mirror's only care, a change at her cloudy temples;
Saying over a poem in the night, does she sense the chill in the moonbeams?
Not far, from here to Fairy Hill.
Bluebird, be quick now, spy me out the road.

第一句的两个“难”字都译成了 hard，我觉得 hard 表示“难过”更好，表示“难得”不如用 difficult。第三句的“丝”字译成 heart's threads，既表示了蚕丝，又表示了内心的相思，译得不错。但是，如果译成 silk 和 love-sick 两个词，那就不但传达了原诗的意美，而且 silk 和 sick 声音和形状都很相似，还能传达原诗的音美和形美。第五句英译者别出心裁，把“晓镜”译成主语主格，仿佛镜子也会为女方担心，这就是把镜子人格化了。但据一般注释，第五、第六句的主语都是女方。从第六句英译文看来，译者也认为“夜吟”的人是女方。如果两句的主语都是女方，那只表示她担心自己变老，担心自己受寒，没有显示双方的爱情。而从前四句看来，主语都是指的男女双方，而以男方为主，所以我认为第五、第六句写的也应该是男女双方。换句话说，诗人早上照镜子的时候，想到的是女方的容颜会不会改变。男方在月下吟诗的时候，女方会不会“心有灵犀一点通”，也感觉到月光的寒冷呢？这样理解，才能表示男女双方心心相印，息息相通，这种刻骨相思才能“到死方尽”“成灰始干”。总而言之，这样才能揭示诗人爱情的深度。

下面我们再来看看李商隐的另一首无题诗：“昨夜星辰昨夜风，画楼西畔桂堂东。身无彩凤双飞翼，心有灵犀一点通。隔座送钩春酒暖，分曹射覆蜡灯红。嗟余听鼓应官去，走马兰台类转蓬。”据刘学锴在《唐诗鉴赏辞典》中说：“李商隐的无题往往着重抒写主人公的心理活动，事件与场景的描叙常常打破一定的时空次序，随着心理活动的流程交错展现。这首诗在这方面表现得相当典型。起联明写昨夜，实际上暗含由今宵到昨夜的情景联想与对比；次联似应续写昨夜，却突然回到今夕相隔的现境；颈联又转为对对方处境的想象，末联则再回到自身。这样大幅度的跳跃，加上实境虚写（如次句），虚境实写（如颈联）等手法的运用，就使得这首采用赋法的无题诗也显得断续无端，变幻迷离，使读者感到困惑了。其实，把它看成古代诗歌中的‘意识流’作品，许多困惑和歧解原是不难解决的。”现在，我们看看 Graham 的译文：

Last night's stars, last night's wind,
By the West wall of the painted house, East of the hall of cassia.
For bodies no fluttering side by side of splendid phoenix wings,

For hearts the one minute thread from root to tip of the magic horn.
At separate tables, played hook-in-the-palm.
The wine of spring warmed.
Teamed as rivals, guessed what the cup hid. The candle flame reddened
Alas, I hear the drum, must go where office summons,
Ride my horse to the Orchid Terrace, the wind-uprooted weed my likeness.

原诗第一、第二句“暗含由今宵到昨夜的情景”，译文却按照原文字面翻译，只写了昨夜，不能使读者联想到今宵。原诗的第三、第四句写“今夕相隔的现境”，用了“彩凤”和“灵犀”两个形象，译文却把“灵犀”译成 magic horn；两句都没有用现在时的动词，使读者看不出这是写今夕的现境。第五、第六句是“对对方处境的想象”，是虚境的实写，译文却变成了实境实写，完全没有理解这首古代“意识流”的作品。因此，我把这首无题诗改译如下：

As last night twinkle stars, as last night blows the breeze
West of the painted bower, east of Cassia Hall.
Having no wings, I can’t fly to you as I please.
Our hearts at one, your ears can hear my inner call.
Maybe you’re playing hook-in-palm and drinking wine
Or guessing what the cup hides under candle red.
Alas! I hear the drum call me to duties mine,
Like rootless weed to Orchid Hall I ride ahead.

现在，我们看看李商隐的第三首无题诗：“来是空言去绝踪，月斜楼上五更钟。梦为远别啼难唤，书被催成墨未浓。蜡照半笼金翡翠，麝熏微度绣芙蓉。刘郎已恨蓬山远，更隔蓬山一万重！”刘学锴说：“这首无题写一位男子对远隔天涯的所爱女子的思念。”“梦为远别”四字是一篇眼目。全诗就是围绕着“梦”来抒写“远别”小情的。不过它没有按照远别—思念—入梦—梦醒的顺序来写，而是先从梦醒时的情景写起，然后再将梦中和梦后、实境与幻觉糅合在一起抒写，最后才点明蓬山重隔，归结到远别之恨。这样的构思，不只是为了避免艺术上的平直，而且是为了更好地突出爱情阻隔的主题。下面我们看看 Graham 的译文：

Coming was an empty promise, you have gone, and left no footprint:
The moonlight slants above the roof, already the fifth watch sounds.
Dreams of remote partings, cries which cannot summon,
Hurrying to finish the letter, ink which will not thicken.
The light of the candle half encloses kingfishers threaded with gold,
The smell of musk comes faintly through embroidered waterlilies.
Young Liu complained that Fairy Hill is far.
Past Fairy Hill, range above range, ten thousand mountains rise.

第一句的“踪”译成 footprint，把虚字译得太实。第二句的“五更”译得准确，但却不能使人想到这是“梦醒时的情景”。第三句“梦为远别”是全诗最重要的四个字，译文“远别”用了复数，那就看不出男子是在思念这一次远别的女子了。第四句主句又没有动词，使读者想不到这是写梦后的实境。第五、第六句写人去楼空的实境，译文中却有楼无人。最后两句用了典故，译者按照字面翻译，不能使读者明白“蓬山重隔”所引起的“远别之恨”。因此，我把这首诗改译如下：

You said you'd come but you are gone and left no trace,
I wake to hear in moonlit tower the fifth watch bell.
In dream my cry couldn't call you back from distant place;
In haste with ink unthickened I cannot write well.
The candlelight illumines half our feathered bed;
The smell of musk still faintly sweetens lotus-screen.
Beyond my reach the far-off fairy mountains spread,
But you're still farther off than fairy mountains green.

李商隐的第四首无题诗是：“飒飒东风细雨来，芙蓉塘外有轻雷。金蟾啮锁烧香入，玉虎牵丝汲井回。贾氏窥帘韩掾少，宓妃留枕魏王才。春心莫共花争发，一寸相思一寸灰！”刘学锴说：“这首无题写一位深锁幽闺的女子追求爱情而失望的痛苦，是一篇刻意伤春之作。”又有人说：这首诗的主题是写一次幽会，最关键的字眼是第三句的“烧香入”和第四句“汲井回”。“烧香”是写晚上，“入”字是写诗人来赴约会；“汲井”是写第二天早上，“回”字是写诗人离开女方回家。现在我们来看看 Graham 是如何译成英文的：

The East wind sighs, the fine rains come:
Beyond the pool of water-lilies, the noise of faint thunder.
A gold toad gnaws the lock. Open it, burn the incense.
A tiger of jade pulls the rope. Draw from the well and escape.
Chia's daughter peeped through the screen when Han the clerk was young,

The goddess of the river left her pillow for the great Prince of Wei.
Never let your heart open with the spring flowers;
One inch of love is an inch of ashes.

从译文看来，不知道原诗是写“伤春”还是幽会。第三、第四句还原就是：“一只金蛤蟆咬着锁，开锁烧香吧。一只玉虎拉着井绳，打上井水逃走吧。”也不知道主语究竟是指男方还是指女方。句中“香”“丝”谐音双关“相思”，看来译者并不知道。原诗第五、第六句是借古写今，借晋朝贾充的女儿和年少的韩寿私通的故事，借曹植和洛神梦中相会的传说，来写诗人和情人的一次幽会。这种借古说今的写法，是中国特有的文化传统，译者按照字面只译出了古代的传说，但西方读者并不知道这两个典故，自然不会联想到诗人的幽会，而只会觉得莫名其妙。因此，我不得不把这首诗改译如下：

The rustling eastern wind came with a drizzle light;
And thunder I faintly rolled beyond the Lotus Pool.
When doors were lock'd and incense burned, I came at night
And went at dawn when windlass pulled up water cool.
You peeped at me first from behind a curtained bower;
I'm left at last but with the pillow of a dame.
Let my desire not bloom and vie with vernal flower!
For inch by inch my heart is consumed by the flame.

总而言之，中国诗的特点是朦胧，诗句往往没有主语，读者可以想象：主语是男方或是女方，或是双方。中文的动词可以写实，也可以写虚；可以写现在，可以写过去，也可以写将来，但在形式上往往看不出分别。这就是说，中文的内容大于形式，可以说一指二，一中见多。此外，中国的文化传统丰富，往往可以借此说彼，这是中文所有而英文所无的言外之意。而英文的特点是精确，一般说来，句子都有主语、动词：动词时态分明，写实要用陈述语气，写虚要用虚拟语气。这就是说，英文的内容和形式相等，只能说一是一，说二是二。因此，把中文译成英文的时候，要用英文之所长，避英文之所短，也就是说，要发挥译文的优势。英文的优势是精确：主语、谓语、时态、语气都有一定的形式。而中文诗的特点恰恰相反：主语、谓语、词性、时态、语气都不分明。如果把中文诗译得形式上和中文诗一样朦胧，那就是舍己之长，用己之短，不但不能吸收中文的优点，反而使译文变得晦涩难懂了。

《中国翻译》1984 年第 3 期第 3 页上说："一首诗是一个意义的有机结构，是一种说话的方式。它反映客观事物，也表达作者的内心世界。……译诗必须分析这个结构，充分理解它，翻译才能神似，近似，如李商隐的《锦瑟》：'锦瑟无端五十弦，一弦一柱思华年。庄生晓梦迷蝴蝶，望帝春心托杜鹃。沧海月明珠有泪，蓝田日暖玉生烟。此情可待成追忆，只是当时已惘然。'"这首诗的意义，我看主要是"思华年"。诗的结构可以分为"起承转合"四联：第一联两句"起"，主要写"思"字；第二联两句"承"，主要写"华年"，第三句写"华年"的迷惘，第四句写"华年"的哀怨；第三联两句"转"，由过去的"华年"转到现在（当时），第五句写当时的哀怨，第六句写当时的迷惘；第四联两句"合"，把过去和现在的迷惘合起来写。如果按照这个理解来分析，可以说第一联是借客观的事物（锦瑟）来表达自己的内心世界（哀怨）。第三句借庄生梦蝴蝶的典故，写作者华年的迷梦，并不是真写庄生，所以庄生不一定要译出来，反而可以增加迷离恍惚之感。第四句说望帝死后，冤魂化为啼血的杜鹃，也是借杜鹃的悲声，写作者的哀怨，所以也不一定要译出“望帝”。第五句主要是用“泪”字写恨，“沧海月明”只是背景。第六句主要是用“烟”字写迷惘，“蓝田日暖”也是背景，翻译不要主次颠倒。第七句“可待”是问话“哪能等到”的意思，如果理解为“将来追想时可以成为美好的回忆”，那就不合原意，和上下文也连不起来。根据我的理解，我把诗译成英文如下：

Why should the sad zither have fifty strings?
Each string, each strain evokes but vanished springs;
Dim morning dream to be a butterfly,
Amorous heart poured out in cuckoo's cry.
In moonlit pearls see tears in mermaid's eyes;
From sunburnt jade in Blue Field let smoke rise!
Such feelings cannot be recalled again;
It seemed long lost even when it was felt then.

《锦瑟》是李商隐象征诗中解释最多的一首。如第二联“庄生晓梦”，有人说是迷惘的梦境，有人说是迷恋于蝴蝶的自由翱翔；“望帝春心”，有人说是爱情，有人说是家国之恨。第三联的“沧海月明”，说的可能是诗人，也可能是鲛人或美人鱼；“蓝田日暖”，多数人说是景语，少数人说是情语，情语最有力的根据是《牡丹亭》第三本第二出《寻梦》中杜丽娘的唱词，说柳梦梅“他倚太湖石，立着咱玉婵娟，待把俺玉山推倒，便日暖玉生烟。”“太湖”就是蓝田，“日”指柳梦梅，“玉”指杜丽娘，“暖生烟”指男欢女爱，巫山云雨，如烟似雾。这个解释有说服力，我就婉转加注把这两联改译如下：

Free morning dream to be a butterfly,
Grief-laden heart poured out in cuckoo's cry.
In moonlit pearls see tears in mermaid's eyes;
With sunburned mirth let blue jade vaporize!

总之，我译李商隐诗，基本是按照钱钟书先生说的：“艺之至者，从心所欲而不逾矩。”钱先生把《论语》中孔子的话引用到艺术上来，我又再把它应用到文学翻译的艺术上。从心所欲，就是充分发挥译者的主观能动性；不逾矩，就是不超越客观规律的范围。这正是中国译者不同于西方译者的一点。西方译者多半进行西方语文之间的翻译，而西方语文如英、法、德、意、西等，据统计约有 90% 有对等词，所以西方提出了对等的翻译理论。而中文和西方语文不同，据统计只有 45% 有对等词。大致说来，如以英文为例，英文精确，说一是一，说二是二，内容等于形式，是科学的语文；中文（尤其是文学语言）精练，往往说一指二，内容可以大于形式，是一种艺术的语言。如果按照对等原则来译，往往词不达意，这就是前面提到的英国译者失败的原因，这点我和美国译者奈达当面谈过，他也提不出反对的意见。其实对等原则主要是“不逾矩”，只能应用于小半英汉文学翻译。

在中英文不能对等的时候，那就要“从心所欲”，发挥译者的主观能动性，不是在译语中选择对等的词汇，而是选择最好的译语表达方式。我译李商隐诗，基本就是根据这个中国学派的文学翻译理论。如果各国译者能了解中西语文的异同，能把中国学派的译论付诸实践，那就可以使世界文化更加丰富多彩，更加光辉灿烂。

许渊冲译李商隐诗选

· · ·

锦　瑟[1]

① 锦瑟：装饰华美的瑟。瑟，拨弦乐器，通常二十五弦。

锦瑟无端五十弦，
一弦一柱思华年。
庄生晓梦迷蝴蝶，
望帝[2]春心托杜鹃。
沧海[3]月明珠有泪[4]，
蓝田日暖玉生烟。
此情可待成追忆，
只是当时已惘然。

② 望帝：《蜀记》中有记载，“昔有人姓杜名宇，王蜀（称王于蜀），号曰望帝。宇死，俗说云宇化为子规。子规，鸟名也。蜀人闻子规鸣，皆曰望帝也。”

③ 沧海：大海。沧，青绿色。

④ 珠有泪：传说南海外有鲛人，其泪能泣珠。

《锦瑟》是李商隐的代表作，历来对这首诗的解释和理解各不相同。该诗不仅使用了多个典故，更重要的是诗外有诗，寓意深长，迷离恍惚，瑰丽缠绵，使历朝历代的读者产生无尽联想，似乎永远说不完，道不尽。

The Sad Zither

Why should the sad zither have fifty strings?
Each string, each strain evokes but vanished springs.
Free morning dream to be a butterfly;
Grief-laden heart poured out in cuckoo's cry.
In moonlit pearls see tears in mermaid's eyes;
With sunburned mirth let blue jade vaporize!
Such feeling cannot be recalled again;
It seemed long lost even when it was felt then.

Note: The music reminds the poet of his freedom like a butterfly, his grief like a lovesick cuckoo, his sorrow to part in tears and his joy in love with sunburnt mirth.

重过圣女祠[1]

① 圣女祠：或以为陈仓（今陕西宝鸡市东）的圣女神祠，或以为托喻女道士居住的道观。

白石岩扉碧藓滋，
上清沦谪得归迟。
一春梦雨常飘瓦，
尽日灵风不满旗。
萼绿华来无定所，
杜兰香[2]去未移时。
玉郎[3]会此通仙籍，
忆向天阶问紫芝。

② 萼绿华，杜兰香：传说中女仙名。

③ 玉郎：道家所称天上掌管神仙名册的官吏。

古代有不少关于天上神女谪降人间的传说，诗人很自然地由眼前这座幽寂的圣女祠产生诸多联想。有人说诗人是托圣女以自寓，借咏圣女而抒发身世沉沦之感慨。诗歌的意境在缥缈中显出沉郁，成功地塑造了一位沦谪不归、幽居无托的圣女形象。

Passing Again the Temple of a Goddess

Over your door of white rock I see green moss grow;
You're banished from the paradise where you can't go.
The dreaming vernal rains with your tiles often play;
The wonder-working wind won't swell your flag all day.
There is no place to shelter fair Emerald Flower,
And fragrant Orchid won't stay here more than an hour.
The Registrar of Jade knows you come from on high.
Let miraculous herb bring you back to the sky!

Note: The poet reveals his sympathy with the Goddess banished from the sky as Adam and Eve driven out of the Paradise after eating of the fruit of wisdom.

霜　月

初闻征雁已无蝉，
百尺楼高水接天。
青女[①]素娥[②]俱耐冷，
月中霜里斗婵娟。

① 青女：主管霜雪的女神。《淮南子·天文训》中有“青女乃出，以降霜雪。”

② 素娥：指嫦娥。

在月白霜清的秋夜，高楼独倚，水光接天，一片澄澈空明。冰肌玉骨的绝代佳人青女和素娥，愈是在宵寒露冷之中，愈是显现出雾鬓风鬟之美。诗人从霜月交辉的夜景里发掘出自然之美，同时也反映了诗人在混浊的现实环境里追求美好、向往光明的深切愿望。

Frost and Moon

No cicadas trill when I first hear wild geese cry;
The high tower overlooks water blend in with the sky.
The Moon Goddess and her Maid of Frost are cold-proof,
They vie in beauty in moonlight over frosty roof.

Note: Seeing the bright moon and frost, the poet imagines the Moon Goddess vying in beauty with her Maid of Frost.

蝉

本以高难饱[1]，
徒劳恨费声。
五更疏欲断，
一树碧无情。
薄宦[2]梗犹泛[3]，
故园芜已平。
烦君最相警，
我亦举家清。

① 高难饱：古人认为蝉栖于高处，餐风饮露，故说“高难饱”。

② 薄宦：官职卑微。

③ 梗犹泛：典出《战国策·齐策》，后以“梗泛”比喻漂泊不定，孤苦无依。梗，指草木的直茎。

首联讲蝉因高洁而食不果腹，悲鸣传恨。次联说蝉的鸣声到五更天亮时已经稀疏得快要断绝，而碧树却置若罔闻，冷酷无情。反映出诗人空有满腹经纶但又怀才不遇的心情。

To the Cicada

High, you can't eat your fill;
In vain you wail and trill.
At dawn you hush your song,
The tree is green for long.
I drift as water flows.
And waste my garden grows.
Thank you for warning due,
I am as poor as you.

Note: The poet compares himself to the poor hungry cicada.

赠刘司户蕡[①]

① 刘蕡：敬宗宝历二年（826 年）进士，博学能文，李商隐对他非常推崇。

江风吹浪动云根，
重碇[②]危樯[③]白日昏。
已断燕鸿初起势，
更惊骚客后归魂。
汉廷急诏谁先入，
楚路高歌自欲翻。
万里相逢欢复泣，
凤巢西隔九重门。

② 碇：系船的石墩。

③ 樯：桅杆。

宣宗大中二年（847 年）春，李商隐与被贬去柳州的刘蕡在长沙一带相遇，李商隐写此诗相赠。诗人由眼前江风的险恶联想到国家的隐忧，像刘蕡这样的国之栋梁居然连遭数贬，希望朝廷能够迅速觉悟，重招刘蕡回朝辅佐，澄清积弊。同时表达了诗人与刘蕡同为天涯沦落人那种欢泣交加的复杂感情。

For an Exiled Friend

Waves surge when blows the wind, clouds rooted in rocks shiver,
The mast and anchor tremble on the darkened river.
How could the northern swan fly up with broken wings?
How could the exiled poet find his Southern springs?
Who would answer the summons of the royal court?
A poet would sing freely the days long or short.
Happy to meet so far from homeland, we shed tears.
When could the phoenix fly to nine celestial spheres?

Note: The poet expresses his sympathy with his exiled friend, wishing him to be recalled like a phoenix or a swan.

悼伤[1]后赴东蜀[2]辟至散关[3]遇雪

① 悼伤：即悼亡，指丧妻。诗人妻子王氏于大中五年秋病故。

② 东蜀：梓州，今四川省绵阳市三台县。

③ 散关：又称大散关，今陕西省宝鸡市西南。

剑外[4]从军远，
无家与寄衣。
散关三尺雪，
回梦旧鸳机[5]。

④ 剑外：剑阁之外，蜀地的代称。

⑤ 鸳机：刺绣的工具。

这首诗反映的是爱妻刚亡，痛楚未定之情境。隆冬之际，作者孑然一身，离家远行，在赴任途中遭遇大雪，行囊单薄，想到自己妻亡家破，无人寄衣御寒，倍加凄苦。

In Snow on the Frontier

So far away on the frontier,
Who'd send me winter garments here?
Buried in snow deep as the gloom,
I miss my deceased on the loom.

Note: The poet missed his deceased wife while going to the frontier in snow.

乐游原[1]

[1] 乐游原：创建于汉宣帝时，本是一处庙苑，称“乐游苑”。只因地势高敞，极目千里，人们遂以“原”呼之。

向晚意不适，
驱车登古原。
夕阳无限好，
只是近黄昏。

诗人驱车登古原，不是为了寻求感慨，而是为了排遣此际的“向晚意不适”的情怀。“夕阳无限好，只是近黄昏”堪称千古名句，描绘了一幅“余晖映照，晚霞满期天，山凝胭脂，气象万千”的场面。

On the Plain of Imperial Tombs

At dusk my heart is filled with gloom,
I drive my cab to ancient tombs.
The setting sun seems drunk with wine,
Magnificent on the decline.

Note: The Plain was a resort for merry-making.

北　齐

（二首其一）

一笑相倾国便亡，
何劳荆棘始堪伤。
小怜玉体横陈夜，
已报周师入晋阳。

《北齐二首》两首诗是通过讽刺北齐后主高纬宠幸冯淑妃荒淫亡国的史实，借古鉴今。

本首借用周幽王宠褒姒而亡国的故事，讽刺“无愁天子”高纬荒淫亡国的故事。

The Downfall of Kingdom Qi

(I)

The king loved less his kingdom than his beauty's smiles.
Could his palace not be buried in briars for miles?
His favored lady lay in bed on full display.
While the foe entered his capital in array.

北 齐

（二首其二）

巧笑知堪敌万几，
倾城最在著戎衣。
晋阳已陷休回顾，
更请君王猎一围。

“巧笑”与“万几”，一女与天下，轻重关系本来一目了然，在高纬眼中，身着戎装的淑妃显然更加迷人。晋州告急，帝妃仍然寻欢作乐，亡国已成定局，无力回天。

The Downfall of Kingdom Qi

(II)

How could a beauty's smile overshadow state affair?

The king was charmed by his lady in hunting dress.

Of his capital in danger he did not care;

He would go hunting one more round nevertheless.

夜雨寄北[1]

① 寄北：写诗寄给北方的人。诗人当时在巴蜀（现在四川省），他的亲友在长安，这首诗表达了诗人对亲友的深刻怀念。

君问归期未有期，
巴山[2]夜雨涨秋池。
何当共剪西窗烛[3]，
却话巴山夜雨时。

② 巴山：指缙云山，在陕西南部和四川东北交界处。这里泛指巴蜀一带。

③ 剪西窗烛：剪烛，剪去燃焦的烛芯，使灯光明亮。这里形容深夜秉烛长谈。

这是李商隐的名篇之一，是诗人身处巴蜀，给远在长安的亲友的回信。纪昀曾点评此诗："作不尽语，不免有做作态，此诗含蓄不露，却只似一气说完，故为高唱。"

Written on a Rainy Night to My Wife in the North

You ask me when I can return, but I don't know;
It rains in western hills and autumn pools overflow.
When can we trim by window side the candlelight
And talk about the western hills in rainy night?

忆　梅

定定①住天涯，

依依向物华。

寒梅最堪恨，

常作去年花②。

① 定定：滞留不动。

② 去年花：指早梅。因为梅花在严冬开放，春天的时候梅花已经凋谢，所以称为“去年花”。

这是李商隐任职于梓州柳仲郢幕府后期之作。寒梅先春而开、望春而凋的特点，或许让诗人想到了自己的人生，早年登第，却薄宦多病，如同先开先谢的寒梅，并不属于春天，未免有落寞飘零之感。

Mume Flowers Recalled

So deep-rooted, so far away,
How I'm attached to spring day!
But I regret cold-proof mume flowers
Beautified only last year's bowers.

Note: The mume flower bloomed in winter.

赠柳

章台[①]从掩映，

郢[②]路更参差。

见说风流极，

来当婀娜时。

桥回行欲断，

堤远意相随[③]。

忍放花如雪，

青楼扑酒旗。

① 章台：汉代京城长安街道名，街旁多柳，唐代时称"章台柳"。

② 郢：战国时期楚国的国都，位于今湖北省荆州市北。

③ 意相随：柳枝傍堤而去，遂意相随。此句既写柳，也写出诗人对柳的不舍。

该诗描绘了春天，柳树从长安到江陵、从北到南，无处不在，秀色千里，生机勃勃的情景。意境优美，让人回味。

To the Willow Tree

I see you vibrate to and fro
And then undulate high and low.
You waft with grace in gentle breeze
And dance so tenderly to please.
No bridge can break you in a line.
Though far away, you still look fine.
Your snow-white catkins beautify
The dancing hall with streamers high.

宿骆氏亭寄怀崔雍崔衮[1]

① 崔雍、崔衮：诗人表叔崔戎的儿子，李商隐的从表兄弟。

竹坞无尘水槛清，
相思迢递[2]隔重城。
秋阴不散霜飞晚，
留得枯荷听雨声。

② 迢递：遥远的样子。

崔雍、崔兖是李商隐的从表兄弟，诗人在秋夜独自一人听雨滴打在枯荷上的声音，一边想念亲人，一边倍感落寞。

For the Cui Brothers at Luo's Pavilion

In the bamboo grove by the clean poolside I stay;
Separated from you by towns, I miss you far away.
The autumn gloom undispersed and late frost remain;
Only the withered lotus listen to the rain.

Note: Passing one night at Luo's Pavilion, the poet thought of The Cui brothers far away and wrote this quatrain which describes his gloomy mood rather than autumn gloom.

风雨

凄凉宝剑篇①，
羁泊欲穷年。
黄叶仍风雨，
青楼②自管弦。
新知遭薄俗，
旧好隔良缘。
心断新丰③酒，
销愁斗几千。

①宝剑篇：唐初郭震所作。《新唐书·郭震传》载，武则天召他谈话，索其诗文，郭即呈上《宝剑篇》，中有句云："非直接交游侠子，亦曾亲近英雄人。何言中路遭捐弃，零落飘沦古岳边。虽复沉埋无所用，犹能夜夜气冲天。"武则天看后大加称赏，立即加以重用。

②青楼：青色的高楼。此处指富贵人家。

③新丰：地名，在今陕西省西安市临潼县东，古时以产美酒闻名。

这首诗反映诗人较落魄的心境，怀才不遇，借酒消愁。

Wind and Rain

As an unused sword I'm as drear.
Oh, when will end my roaming year?
Yellow leaves fall in winds and rains;
Green mansions play strings and sing strains.
My new friends are left in the cold;
Can I often meet my peers old?
How I long for nectar divine
To drown my lonely grief in wind!

Note: The poet shows that he has more talent than recognition.

梦　泽

梦泽悲风动白茅[1]，
楚王[2]葬尽满城娇。
未知歌舞能多少，
虚减宫厨为细腰。

① 白茅：茅草。春夏间抽生有银白色丝毛状花穗。

② 楚王：指楚灵王。《韩非子·二柄》："楚灵王好细腰，而国中多饿人"。《后汉书马廖传》："楚王好细腰。宫中多（遍）饿死（殍）。"

本篇是诗人途经梦泽时所作，一望无际的白茅，好似被埋葬的嫔妃宫娥采女的哀旗。楚灵王喜欢女子细腰，宫嫔们为投其所好饥饿节食，却消瘦而死，不禁让人惋惜。

The Dreaming Lake

On Dreaming Lake in biting wind pale grasses shiver;
Like slender dancers buried like waves in the river.
How long could they delight the monarch in the South?
The royal cook might give less food to rosebud mouth.

Note: The King of Chu（楚王）loved the slender waist of dancers and many Chu dancers died of hunger.

寄令狐郎中[1]

① 令狐郎中：即令狐绹，当时在朝中任考功郎中。

嵩云秦树久离居，

双鲤[2]迢迢一纸书。

休问梁园[3]旧宾客，

茂陵[4]秋雨病相如。

② 双鲤：指书信。古乐府《饮马长城窟行》："客从远方来，遗我双鲤鱼。呼童烹鲤鱼，中有尺素书。"

③ 梁园：汉梁孝王刘武的园林，此喻指楚幕、司马相如等文士都曾客游梁园。比喻自己昔年游于令狐门下。

④ 茂陵：在今陕西省咸阳市兴平县，因汉武帝陵墓而得名。司马相如因患病，家居茂陵，作者此时也卧病于洛阳。

这是作者于 845 年在洛阳回寄给长安故友令狐绹的一首诗，率真诚恳。嵩、秦分指诗人所在的洛阳和令狐绹所在的长安。

For a Friend

We're severed long by northern cloud and western trees;
Your letter's sent to quench my thirst from far away.
Don't ask about your friend in lonely garden, please!
Just read the poet sick with rainy autumn day!

哭刘蕡

上帝深宫闭九阍[1]，
巫咸[2]不下问衔冤。
黄陵[3]别后春涛隔，
湓浦[4]书来秋雨翻。
只有安仁[5]能作诔[6]，
何曾宋玉解招魂。
平生风义兼师友，
不敢同君哭寝门。

① 九阍：九天之门，比喻帝王的宫门。

② 巫咸：传说中的古代神巫。

③ 黄陵：在今湖南省岳阳市湘阴县北。《哭刘司户蕡》也有："去年相送地，春雪满黄陵。"

④ 湓浦：指江州，今江西省九江市。从江州传来刘蕡的死讯，正是秋雨降落之时。

⑤ 安仁：西晋潘岳的字，擅长写作哀诔文。

⑥ 诔：古代叙述死者生前事迹，表示哀悼的文体。

诗人敬慕刘蕡才华，与刘蕡亦师亦友，虽然不是旧交故友，但是肝胆相照，想不到黄陵一别，竟成永诀。自己对友人的逝世无能为力，不能复其魂魄，让刘蕡死而复生，只能作悼词哀悼亡友。

Elegy on Liu Fen

Closed are the palace gates of the celestial spheres;
No witch is sent to inquire if you're right or wrong.
Spring tides have severed us since we parted in tears,
Your death turns autumn rain weeping all day long.
I would turn raindrops into words to mourn for you.
Could the poet call back the soul of my compeer?
I admire you as an old friend and teacher new.
How could I weep for you in and out, far and near?

Note: It was believed that a witch would be sent from the celestial spheres to right the wrong in the human world. The poet in line 6 refers to Song Yu（宋玉）who would call back the soul of Qu Yuan（屈原）of the 3rd Century B. C.

杜司勋[1]（牧）

① 杜司勋：即杜牧。

高楼风雨感斯文，
短翼差池[2]不及群。
刻意伤春复伤别，
人间惟有杜司勋。

② 差池：指燕飞时尾羽参差不齐。出自《诗经·国风·邶风·燕燕》："燕燕于飞，差池其羽。"

风雨之日，李商隐登楼感叹杜牧诗文，欣赏其才华、悲叹其命运，既是在说杜牧，也是在说自己。

For Du Mu

Your verse exhales spring wind and rain in tower high,
Left far behind with my short swallow wings, I sigh.
At parting spring and parting with friends old and new,
Who in the world is drowned in deeper grief than you?

Note: This is a eulogy to Du Mu（杜牧）, poet well known for his parting poems.

杜工部蜀中离席

人生何处不离群[1]，
世路干戈惜暂分。
雪岭未归天外使[2]，
松州[3]犹驻殿前军。
座中醉客延醒客，
江上晴云杂雨云。
美酒成都堪送老，
当垆[4]仍是卓文君。

① 离群：《札记·檀弓》："吾离群索居，亦已久矣。"

② 天外使：指远在雪岭那边的朝廷使臣。

③ 松州：今四川省阿坝藏族羌族自治州松潘县。

④ 当垆：烤酒。卓文君和司马相如在成都，文君当垆（烤酒），相如涤器（买酒）。

人生经常因各种事情无奈别离。该诗描绘了战乱时期诗人与朋友惜别的感伤，同时也表达了诗人忧国忧民的思想感情。

Would Du Fu not leave the Farewell Feast?

Could we have no meeting and parting in our life?
But parting would bring grief in time of war and strife.
The peace envoy has not come back from the frontiers;
Our forts are guarded still by royal cavaliers.
The drunken in the feast talk to the sober loud,
While on the river float fleecy cloud and dark cloud.
"Won't good wine intoxicate you all your life long.
If accompanied by a beauty's sweeter song?

Note: Imitating Du Fu (杜甫), the poet says that parting in time of war would bring more woe than in time of peace.

隋　宫[1]

（其一）

① 隋宫：指隋炀帝杨广在江都（今江苏省扬州市）所建的行宫。

紫泉[2]宫殿锁烟霞，
欲取芜城作帝家。
玉玺不缘归日角，
锦帆[3]应是到天涯。
于今腐草无萤火，
终古垂杨有暮鸦。
地下若逢陈后主，
岂宜重问后庭花。

② 紫泉：即紫渊，长安河名。

③ 锦帆：隋炀帝所乘的龙舟，其帆用华丽的宫锦制成。

隋炀帝杨广是历史上有名的荒淫昏暴的皇帝。他在位的14年里，居京不足一年，大多时间都在外淫游。此诗即写隋炀帝穷奢极欲的生活，以借古讽今。该诗采用兴比手法，用典融化无痕，写得灵动含蓄，音节铿锵，跌宕有致，在咏史诗中独树一帜。

The Sui Palace

(I)

The Palace of Purple Spring lost in rainbow cloud
Might be replaced by new one in riverside town.
Were the emperor not overthrown by the crowd,
His royal ship might sail to new sky's end unknown.
But now no fireflies overspread the withered grass;
Only dark crows perch on his weeping willow trees.
If he met underground his captive king, alas!
Could the sweet song of their palace flowers still please?

Note: This is a satire against the last emperor of the Sui Dynasty（隋炀帝）who would go south to spend a luxurious life in a riverside town if he were not overthrown by the Tang（唐）army. The captive king refers to the last king of Chen Dynasty（陈后主）who was enjoying music of his favorite songstress when the Sui（隋）army entered his capital.

隋　宫

（隋堤）

乘兴南游不戒严，
九重[1]谁省[2]谏书函[3]。
春风举国裁宫锦[4]，
半作障泥[5]半作帆。

① 九重：指皇帝居住的深宫。
② 省：明察，懂得。
③ 谏书函：给皇帝的谏书。
④ 宫锦：供皇家使用的高级锦缎。
⑤ 障泥：马鞯，垫在马鞍的下面，两边下垂至马镫，用来挡泥土。

隋炀帝的腐败与昏暴，在历代皇帝中尤为突显。此诗一二句谓其轻狂和残暴，三四句谓其多次南游，耗尽民脂民膏。

将此诗与七律《隋宫》诗对读，会感到律诗与绝句诗的不同。律诗篇长，适于铺展，而绝句句数少，不得不节省笔墨，充分发挥含蓄的功效。

The Sui Palace

(II)

The pleasure-seeking monarch toured the South at will.

Who dare alert him in the ninth celestial sphere?

People were forced to weave brocade through the mill

But half was used as mudguard and half as sail too dear.

Note: This is another satire against the last emperor of the Sui Dynasty (隋炀帝) who forced people to weave brocade for his carriages and ships and punished with death those who dared to alert him.

二月二日[①]

① 二月二日：蜀地风俗，二月二日为踏青节。

二月二日江上行，
东风[②]日暖闻吹笙[③]。
花须[④]柳眼[⑤]各无赖[⑥]，
紫蝶黄蜂俱有情。
万里忆归元亮井[⑦]，
三年从事亚夫营[⑧]。
新滩莫悟游人意，
更作风檐夜雨声。

② 东风：春风。

③ 笙：一种管乐器。

④ 花须：花蕊，因花蕊细长如须，所以称为花须。

⑤ 柳眼：柳叶的嫩芽，因嫩芽如人睡眼方展，所以称为柳眼。

⑥ 无赖：本指人多诈狡狯，这里形容花柳都在任意地生长，从而撩起游人的羁愁。

⑦ 元亮井：这里指故里。元亮，东晋诗人陶渊明的字。

⑧ 亚夫营：这里借指柳仲郢的军幕。亚夫，即周亚夫，汉代的将军。

诗的首句“二月二日江上行”，点明踏青节江上春游。和煦的春风，温暖的旭日，散发着浓浓的春意。春江水涨，新滩流水在一般游春者听来，自然是欢畅悦耳的春之歌；但在思归不得的作者耳中，却像是午夜檐间风雨的凄凉之声。

The Second Day of the Second Moon

On second day of second moon I sail on stream.
The vernal wind brings warmth and I hear flutist sing.
Red flowers have no heart and green willows no dream,
But purple butterflies and golden bees love spring.
How can I live from my homeland so far apart?
In willow camp I've done my duty for three years.
The rippling stream can't understand a roamer's heart;
The night rain dripping from old roof assails my ears.

Note: This poem contrasts the beauty of spring with the homesickness of the poet.

筹笔驿

猿鸟[1]犹疑畏简书，
风云常为护储胥[2]。
徒令上将挥神笔，
终见降王[3]走传车。
管[4]乐[5]有才终不忝，
关张无命欲何如？
他年锦里经祠庙，
梁父吟[6]成恨有馀。

① 猿鸟犹疑畏简书：诸葛亮治军以严明称，这里意谓至今连鱼鸟还在惊畏他的简书。简书，指军令，古人将文字写在竹简上。

② 储胥：指军用的篱栅。

③ 降王：指后主刘禅。

④ 管：管仲。春秋时齐相，曾佐齐桓公成就霸业。

⑤ 乐：乐毅。战国时人，燕国名将，曾大败强齐。

⑥ 梁父吟：古乐府中一首葬歌。《三国志》说诸葛亮躬耕陇亩，好为梁父吟，借以抒发空怀济世之心，聊以吟诗以自遣。

筹笔驿位于四川省广元市北，蜀诸葛亮武侯出师伐魏时，尝驻军于此筹划军机。宣宗大中十年（856年）冬，李商隐辞职返京途经筹笔驿，有感于诸葛亮雄才大略却功业未竟，而写下这首享有盛名的怀古诗，叹息诸葛亮功业未成的千古遗憾。

The Premier's Military Station

Monkeys and birds have not forgot the Premier's order;
Still wind and cloud would screen and shield his ancient border.
In vain had he made prodigious strategic plan;
At last the captive king was gone in prison van.
He had the talent of wise marshals in their prime.
What could he do with generals lost before their time?
When people visit his temple in later days,
Their regret would outlast the song sung in his praise.

Note: This is a eulogy of Premier Zhuge Liang (诸葛亮) of the Kingdom of Shu (蜀). The Kingdom lost many generals and its last ruler became a captive.

无　题

（二首其一）

昨夜星辰[1]昨夜风，
画楼[2]西畔桂堂东。
身无彩凤双飞翼，
心有灵犀[3]一点通。
隔座送钩[4]春酒暖，
分曹[5]射覆[6]蜡灯红。
嗟余听鼓应官去，
走马兰台[7]类断蓬。

① 星辰：众星，星之通称。

② 画楼：指彩绘华丽的高楼。

③ 灵犀：犀角中心的髓质像一条白线贯通上下，借喻双方心灵的感应和暗通。

④ 隔座送钩：一队用一钩藏在手内，隔座传送，使另一队猜钩所在，以猜中为胜。

⑤ 分曹：分组。

⑥ 射覆：把东西放在瓯、盂等器具下使人猜。

⑦ 兰台：秘书省的别称。《旧唐书·职官志》："秘书省，龙朔（唐高宗年号）初改为兰台。"当时李商隐在做秘书省校书郎。

"身无彩凤双飞翼，心有灵犀一点通"可谓千古名句——尽管自己身上没有彩凤那样的双翅能够飞越阻隔，与对方相会，但彼此的心，却像犀角一样，自有一线相通，深挚缠绵。

Unnamed

(I)

As last night twinkle stars, as last night blows the breeze,
West of the painted bower, east of Cassia Hall.
Having no wings, I can't fly to you as I please;
Our hearts at one, your ears can hear my inner call.
Maybe you're playing hook in palm and drinking wine
Or guessing what the cup hides under candle red.
Alas! I hear the drum call me to duties mine;
Like rootless weed to Orchid Hall I ride ahead.

Note: The poet who worked in Orchid Hall and lived in Cassia Hall recalled the night spent together with an unnamed mistress and imagined what she was doing on his lonely night, for their hearts were communicative.

无　题

（四首其一）

来是空言去绝踪，
月斜楼上五更钟。
梦为远别啼难唤，
书被催成墨未浓。
蜡照半笼[①]金翡翠，
麝[②]熏微度绣芙蓉。
刘郎[③]已恨蓬山远，
更隔蓬山[④]一万重。

① 半笼：半映。指烛光隐约，不能全照床上被褥。

② 麝：本动物名，即香獐，其体内的分泌物可作香料。这里即指香气。

③ 刘郎：相传东汉时刘晨、阮肇一同入山采药，遇二女子，邀至家，留半年乃还乡。后也以此典喻“艳遇”。

④ 蓬山：蓬莱山，指仙境。

关于这周诗歌有很多的解读，但不管是何种解读，我们都能深深地感受到该诗背后的热烈情感。该诗用典巧妙，辞藻华丽，描写极为细腻，彰显诗人深有造诣的心力与笔力。

Unnamed

(I)

You said you'd come, but you are gone and left no trace;
I wake to hear in moonlit tower the fifth watch bell.
I dream my cry could not call you back from distant place;
In haste with ink unthickened I cannot write well.
The candlelight illuminates half our broidered bed;
The smell of musk still faintly sweeten lotus screen.
Beyond my reach the far-off fairy mountain spread,
But you're still farther off than fairy mountains green.

Note: The poet describes his longing for a lover far away.

无　题

（四首其二）

飒飒东风细雨来，
芙蓉塘[①]外有轻雷。
金蟾[②]啮锁烧香入，
玉虎[③]牵丝汲井回。
贾氏[④]窥帘韩掾[⑤]少，
宓妃[⑥]留枕魏王才。
春心莫共花争发，
一寸相思一寸灰。

① 芙蓉塘：荷塘。

② 金蟾：金蛤蟆。古时在锁头上的装饰。啮：咬。

③ 玉虎：用玉石作装饰的井上辘轳，形如虎状。

④ 贾氏：西晋贾充的次女。她在门帘后窥见韩寿，爱悦他年少俊美，两人私通。贾氏以皇帝赐贾充的异香赠寿，被贾充发觉，遂以女嫁给韩寿。

⑤ 韩掾：指韩寿。韩曾为贾充的掾属。

⑥ 宓妃：古代传说，伏羲氏之女名宓妃，溺死于洛水上，成为洛神。

此诗通过回忆前情、抒发因追求爱情而失望的痛苦，再现了女子与情郎幽会之短暂、相思之悲苦的动人情景。诗人巧妙地将比喻、用典、对照融为一体，把抽象的幽思和爱情具体化、形象化，但终而使美好爱情毁灭，别具匠心地塑造了一种动人心魄的悲剧美。

Unnamed

(II)

The rustling eastern wind came with a drizzle light,
And thunder faintly rolled beyond the lotus pool.
When doors were locked and incense burned, I came at night,
And went at dawn when windlass pulled up water cool.
You peeped at me first from behind a curtained bower;
I'm left at last but with the pillow of a dame.
Let my desire not bloom and vie with vernal flower!
For inch by inch my heart is consumed by the flame

Note: The poet describes a rendezvous of two lovers. The wind and rain are symbols of love-making. It was said that during the rendezvous of the Southern King (楚襄王) and the Goddess of Mount Witch (巫山神女), the Goddess would bring fresh shower for the thirsting flower, which becomes the symbol of love-making. The faintly rolling thunder may allude to the rolling royal carriage and the lotus pond to the rendezvous. The lover comes at night and leaves at dawn. Line 5 describes their first meeting as love at first sight and line 6 their parting as that of Prince of literary fame (曹植) and the Goddess of River Luo (洛水女神) who left him only a pillow. This shows that a good beginning may not end well, so it might be better not to inflame the desire.

无　题

（四首其四）

何处哀筝[1]随急管，

樱花永巷垂杨岸。

东家老女[2]嫁不售，

白日当天三月半。

溧阳公主[3]年十四，

清明暖后同墙看。

归来展转到五更，

梁间燕子闻长叹。

①哀筝：高亢清亮的筝声。

②东家老女：宋玉《登徒子好色赋》："臣里之美者，莫若臣东家之子。"此处暗示这位老女是容华美艳的姑娘，之所以不嫁，并非貌不美，只是家境贫寒。

③溧阳公主：梁简文帝的女儿。这里泛指贵家女子。

此诗先写东家老女婚嫁失时，自伤迟暮；与之对比，贵家女子生活得得意美满。同样是阳春三月，丽日当天，一边是年长难嫁，形单影只；一边却是少年得志，夫妇同游。东家老女归来后在漫长的深夜中辗转难眠，哀叹命运。

Unnamed

(IV)

From where come happy song and lyric full of gloom?
From willowy shore and long lane where cherries bloom.
The eastern villager's poor beauty is not wed.
Though like the sun of late spring shining overhead.
The rich and noble princess is only fourteen;
Suitors on mourning day break walls and willow screen.
How could the old maid not toss in bed deep in night?
Even swallows on the beam would sigh for her plight.

Note: This untitled poem contrasts a lonely poor old maid with a rich young princess who had many suitors.

王十二兄[①]与畏之[②]员外相访见招小饮时予以悼亡日近[③]不去因寄

① 王十二兄：诗人岳父王茂元之子。

② 畏之：诗人的连襟韩瞻。

③ 悼亡日近：指诗人的妻子去世不久。

谢傅[④]门庭旧末行，
今朝歌管属檀郎[⑤]。
更无人处帘垂地，
欲拂尘时簟竟床。
嵇氏幼男[⑥]犹可悯，
左家娇女[⑦]岂能忘。
秋霖腹疾[⑧]俱难遣，
万里西风夜正长。

④ 谢傅：东晋大臣谢安，死后赠太傅，这里以谢傅门庭借指岳父王茂元家。

⑤ 檀郎：晋潘岳小字檀奴，貌美，人称檀郎，唐人常以此谓为女婿。

⑥ 嵇氏幼男：晋代嵇绍，为嵇康之子，十岁丧母。

⑦ 左家娇女：晋代大诗人左思有二女，作有《娇女诗》。

⑧ 秋霖腹疾：指淫雨引起的腹泻。

宣宗大中五年（851 年）春夏之交，李商隐的妻子王氏病故，诗人遭受巨大打击。这年秋天，商隐的内兄王十二和连襟韩瞻邀请李商隐前往王家小饮。诗人因王氏亡故未久，心绪不好，没有应邀。之后写了这首诗寄给王、韩二人，解释不能前去的原因，抒写了对王氏深切的悼亡之情。

An Invitation Declined

Thank you for your invitation to wine,
But this pleasure today I must decline.
Who'd help me to draw my curtains apart
Or dust my lonely bed with broken heart?
Who would take care of my motherless son
And my daughter who lost her dearest one?
Could I be dried up after drenching rain?
The cold windy night will long long remain.

Note: The poet declined the invitation of his brothers-in-law after the mourning day of his deceased wife.

落　花

高阁客竟去[1]，

小园花乱飞。

参差[2]连曲陌[3]，

迢递[4]送斜晖。

肠断未忍扫，

眼穿仍欲归。

芳心[5]向春尽，

所得是沾衣[6]。

①客竟去：客人竟然都离去了。

②参差：错落不齐的样子。

③曲陌：曲折的小径。

④迢递：高远的样子。

⑤芳心：这里既指花的精神灵魂，又指怜爱花的人的心境。

⑥沾衣：既指落花依依沾在人的衣服之上，又指怜爱花的人伤心而抛洒的泪滴。

这是一首专咏落花的咏物诗，将望眼欲穿的婉委悲思与春去花落的婉转飘零融成一片，婉转附物，惆怅切情。

Fallen Flowers

My guest has left my tower high;
My garden flowers pell-mell fly.
Here and there over the winding way
They say good bye to parting day.
I won't sweep them with broken heart,
But wish they would not fall apart.
Their love with spring won't disappear,
Each dewdrop turns into a tear.

Note: The poet describes his gloom on seeing falling flowers.

柳

曾逐东风[①]拂舞筵[②]，
乐游春苑断肠天。
如何肯到清秋日[③]，
已带斜阳又带蝉。

①东风：指春风。

②舞筵：歌舞的筵席。

③清秋日：明净爽朗的秋天。晋殷仲文《南州桓公九井作》诗："独有清秋日，能使高兴尽。"

该诗写的是秋日之柳，诗人先追想春日的情景，然后再回到眼前的秋日之柳。全诗言少意丰，隐而不露，含蓄委婉，不着一个"柳"字，却句句有柳，抒发了作者对稀疏衰落的秋柳的悲叹之情。

To the Willow

Having caressed the dancers in the vernal breeze.
You're ravished amid the merry-making trees.
How can you wait until clear autumn days are done
To shrill like poor cicadas in the setting sun?

Note: The willow is a symbol of the poet himself who would have changed the face of the world while young but could not realize his ideal while old just as the willow swaying in spring but shrilling in autumn like a poor cicada on the branch of a willow tree.

为 有

为有云屏[①]无限娇，

凤城[②]寒尽怕春宵。

无端嫁得金龟婿，

辜负香衾事早朝。

①云屏：云母屏风。雕饰着云母图案的屏风，古代皇家或富贵人家所用。

②凤城：此指京城。

这篇以诗开头“为有”二字为题，实则也是一首“无题”诗。一位富家女子，嫁得意中人，夫妻恩爱。可惜偏偏丈夫要经常早起上朝，引起妻子的抱怨，心理刻画十分细致，含蓄深沉。

A Nobleman's Wife

Behind the screen his wife is charming without peer;
But she's afraid the vernal night should be too short.
Why should she be wed to her noble lord so dear?
At early dawn he'd leave her pillow for the court.

Note: This quatrain describes the sorrow of a nobleman's wife whose lord should rise early to go to court.

无　题

相见时难别亦难，
东风无力百花残。
春蚕到死丝方尽，
蜡炬成灰泪始干。
晓镜但愁云鬓①改，
夜吟应觉月光寒②。
蓬山③此去无多路，
青鸟④殷勤为探看。

① 云鬓：女子多而美的头发，这里比喻青春年华。

② 月光寒：指夜渐深。

③ 蓬山：蓬莱山，传说中海上仙山，指仙境。

④ 青鸟：神话中为西王母传递音讯的信使。

这曾经被解读成一首写离别相思、两情至死不渝的爱情诗。全诗绮靡浓艳，体贴人情，凄迷若幻，情韵悠长，从头至尾都熔铸着痛苦、失望而又缠绵、执着的感情。

Unnamed

It's difficult for us to meet and hard to part;
The east wind is too weak to revive flowers dead.
Spring silkworm till its death spins silk from lovesick heart;
Candles only when burned up have no tears to shed.
At dawn I'm grieved to think your mirrored hair turn grey;
At night you would feel cold while I croon by moonlight.
To the three fairy hills it is not a long way.
Would the blue birds oft fly to see you on the height?

Note: The poet describes his love for an unnamed sweetheart. He cannot meet her again with whom he parted, just as the weak east wind cannot revive dead flowers. But he will love her just as the silkworm will spin silk until its death or the candle will shed light until it is burned out. He could see her in his mirror and she could hear him chant his verse in moonlight. At last, he would ask the blue birds to see her in the fairy hills.

碧　城

（三首其一）

碧城①十二曲阑干，
犀辟尘埃②玉辟寒。
阆苑③有书多附鹤④，
女床无树不栖鸾。
星沉海底当窗见，
雨过河源隔座看。
若是晓珠明又定，
一生长对水晶盘。

① 碧城：道教传为元始天尊之所居，后引申指仙人、道隐、女冠居处。

② 犀辟尘埃：指女冠华贵高雅，头上插着犀角簪，一尘不染。

③ 阆苑：神仙居处。此借指道观。

④ 附鹤：道教传仙道以鹤传书，称鹤信。

《碧城》（三首）是李商隐诗最难懂的篇章之一，历来众说纷纭。三首诗都用第一首诗开头的“碧城”二字为题，实际上也是无题诗。本篇为三首的第一首，采用象征、暗示、双关、用典等表现方法，乍一读去，似觉恍惚迷离，难明所指。然而只要反复体味，仍能曲径通幽，捕捉到诗的旨趣。

Green Rainbow Cloud

(I)

Twelve balustrades wind in the town of rainbow cloud,
Where rhino and jade keep dust and cold air away.
The crane would send the fairy's love to phoenix proud,
There is no tree by the wall where lovebirds stay.
Stars seen before the window sink deep into the night.
And bring showers for thirsting flowers by the stream.
If the pearl of the morning should be ever bright,
How could the fairy face the crystal moon in dream?

Note: This is a poem about the love of fairies who live above the rainbow clouds and for whom the crane will bring love letter to the phoenix. The stars bringing showers for thirsting flowers allude to the love-making of the fairies.

端　居[1]

① 端居：闲居。

远书归梦两悠悠，
只有空床敌素秋[2]。
阶下青苔与红树，
雨中寥落月中愁。

② 素秋：秋天的代称。

这是李商隐的一首思乡之作，表达出浓郁的家乡情怀，抒发了诗人极度孤寂、悲愁的心境，以悲哀的艺术引起人们心灵的震颤和同情的眼泪。

Homesickness

Nor dream nor letter come from home, I'm at a loss,
Only an empty bed against an autumn night.
Below the steps red maple leaves confront green moss,
What loneliness in rain and what grief in moonlight!

咏　史

（二首其一）

北湖南埭[①]水漫漫，
一片降旗百尺竿[②]。
三百年[③]间同晓梦，
钟山[④]何处有龙盘[⑤]。

①北湖南埭：统指玄武湖。北湖，即金陵（今江苏省南京市）玄武湖。南埭，即鸡鸣埭，在玄武湖边。埭，水闸，土坝。

②一片降旗百尺竿：刘禹锡《金陵怀古》："一片降旗出石头。"指吴主孙皓投降晋龙骧将军王浚，也指陈后主投降隋庐州总管韩擒虎。

③三百年：指东吴、东晋、宋、齐、梁、陈六朝建国年代的约数。

④钟山：金陵紫金山。

⑤龙盘：形容山势如盘龙。

此诗题目已经标明，是一首咏史诗，辛辣地讽刺南朝帝王的兴败没落。

On History

(I)

Water shimmers in Northern Lake by Southern Tower
All kings surrendered with white flags to a new power.
Three hundred years have passed like a dream one and all,
No Mount Dragon could keep kingdoms from their downfall.

Note: The Northern Lake, Southern Tower, Mount Coiling Dragon were all in the vicinity of the capital, but neither mountain nor river could keep kingdoms from their downfall.

日　射

日射纱窗风撼扉，
香罗[①]拭手春事[②]违。
回廊四合掩寂寞，
碧鹦鹉对红蔷薇。

① 香罗：对手帕的美称。罗，丝织品。
② 春事：春光，喻青春年华。

阳光照射纱窗，风摇窗扉，闺中人盥洗完毕，无所事事，时间就此流逝。三四句写院中回廊环抱，空锁忧愁，不甚寂寥，一片凄凉生悲愁，唯见蔷薇自放，鹦鹉无语，相对无言。

Loneliness

Sunlight on window screen, the door shivers in breeze;
Her handkerchief waves adieu to spring ill at ease.
None knows her loneliness the corridors enclose,
She hears an emerald parrot talk to a rose.

齐宫词

永寿[①]兵来夜不扃[②]，
金莲[③]无复印中庭。
梁台[④]歌管三更罢，
犹自风摇九子铃[⑤]。

① 永寿：殿名。南齐废帝萧宝卷宠爱潘妃，修建永寿、玉寿、神仙等宫殿，四壁都用黄金涂饰。

② 扃：关宫门。501年，雍州刺史萧衍（即后来的梁武帝）率兵攻入南齐京城建康（今江苏省南京市），齐的叛臣王珍国等做内应，将宫门打开，萧衍带兵进入，萧宝卷被杀。

③ 金莲：萧宝卷凿金为莲花贴地，令潘妃行其上曰："此步步生莲花也。"

④ 梁台：晋、宋间称朝廷禁省为台。梁台即梁宫，在今南京玄武湖畔。

⑤ 九子铃：挂在宫殿寺庙檐前作装饰用的铃，用金、玉等材料制成。

前两句写南齐废帝荒淫无度，身死国亡；后两句写梁代君主同样荒淫，其结局也没有什么不同。该诗以古喻今，抨击了当朝的骄奢淫逸与腐朽没落，讽刺辛辣，令人慨叹，务须戒鉴。

Song of the Ancient Palace

When the foe came at night, unguarded was the palace door;
In mid-court golden lotus blooms left trace no more.
At midnight the new emperor did not stop singing;
The ancient palace bells in the breeze still kept ringing.

Note: In 501 the last emperor of the Qi (齐) Dynasty was enjoying the dance of golden lotus blooms when the Liang (梁) army came and killed the last Qi emperor and founded the Liang Dynasty. But the new emperor of Liang still enjoyed music and dance as the emperor of Qi, so the Liang Dynasty was soon overthrown and replaced by the Chen (陈) Dynasty.

十一月中旬至扶风[①]界见梅花

① 扶风：即今陕西省宝鸡市扶风县。

匝路亭亭艳，
非时裛裛[②]香。
素娥惟与月，
青女不饶霜。
赠远虚盈手，
伤离适断肠。
为谁成早秀[③]，
不待作年芳[④]。

② 裛裛：气味郁盛的样子。

③ 早秀：早开的梅花。

④ 作年芳：为迎接新年而开花芬芳。

首联写梅花提前绽放，繁艳清香；颔联写嫦娥助以清辉，青女不减霜威，更使梅花显得凄清；颈联写满手的梅花不知赠予谁，离别的哀愁令人断肠；尾联写梅花未及报春，提前香艳，为谁早早地绽开呢？此诗以梅花自喻，慨叹自己虚成早秀、孤凄不遇的悲哀。

Mume Blossoms by the Roadside

Fair by the roadside I see you,
Fragrant before the season due.
The moon will not have her light lost;
The fairy will bite you with frost.
You'll be given to parting friends
With broken heart without an end.
Why should you so early appear
Before the blossom-coming year?

Note: Neither the moon nor the fairy love the mume blossoms blooming by the roadside in winter.

汉宫词

青雀[①]西飞竟未回，
君王长在集灵台[②]。
侍臣最有相如渴，
不赐金茎露[③]一杯。

① 青雀：指青鸟，《山海经》中提到的西王母所使之神鸟。

② 集灵台：汉时台名。

③ 金茎露：承露盘中的露，是汉武帝在建章宫神明台所立的金铜仙人承露盘接贮的“云表之露”。

李商隐一生经历了唐宪、穆、敬、文、武、宣六朝，此时的唐朝正走向衰败。本诗以汉宫轶事为题引，借西王母携青鸟会见汉武帝，许诺三年后再来而未至的神话故事，巧妙地表达了像诗人这样渴求为帝王尽忠效力的侍臣得不到信任和重用的遗憾、失望和凄楚之情。

The Han Palace

The blue bird did not bring elixir from the sky;
In vain the monarch waited in his tower high.
His talented poet thirsty for drink divine
Was never given a drop of immortal wine.

Note: This is a satire against the Martial Emperor of the Han Dynasty who sent blue birds to bring back elixir from the sky, but did not give a drop of the divine drink to his thirsty talented poet.

马嵬[1]

（二首其一）

① 马嵬：即马嵬坡，杨贵妃陨落之地，在今陕西省兴平市西。

冀马[2]燕犀[3]动地来，
自埋红粉自成灰。
君王若道能倾国，
玉辇[4]何由过马嵬。

② 冀马：古冀州之北所产的马，泛指马。

③ 燕犀：燕地制造的犀甲，泛指坚固的铠甲。

④ 玉辇：天子所乘之车，以玉为饰。

马嵬事变发生于唐玄宗天宝十四载（755年）安史之乱爆发之后。天宝十五载六月，安禄山攻破潼关，唐玄宗弃长安奔蜀，行至距长安百余里的马嵬坡时，守护皇帝的禁军启请诛杨国忠父子，之后，禁军仍不散，迫使玄宗诛死杨贵妃。如果玄宗能一早知道好色荒政有亡国的危险，那么后来的悲剧又从何谈起呢？

On Lady Yang's Death

(I)

When rebels came from north, trembled the western land;

The Beauty's ashes were buried by Royal hand.

If the emperor had foreseen his own downfall,

He'd not have lost his throne and his Beauty at all.

马　嵬

（二首其二）

海外徒闻更九州，
他生未卜此生休。
空闻虎旅[①]传宵柝[②]，
无复鸡人[③]报晓筹。
此日六军同驻马，
当时七夕笑牵牛。
如何四纪[④]为天子，
不及卢家有莫愁[⑤]。

① 虎旅：指跟随玄宗入蜀的禁军。

② 宵柝：又名金柝，夜间报更的刁斗。

③ 鸡人：皇宫中报时的卫士。

④ 四纪：四十八年。岁星十二年一周天为一纪，唐玄宗在位四十五年，约为四纪。

⑤ 莫愁：古洛阳女子，嫁为卢家妇，婚后生活幸福。萧衍《河中之水歌》："河中之水向东流，洛阳女儿名莫愁。莫愁十三能织绮，十四采桑南陌头。十五嫁作卢家妇，十六生儿字阿侯。卢家兰室桂为梁，中有郁金苏合香。"

诗人巧用倒叙和追忆的笔法将唐玄宗在马嵬坡的悲惨处境描述得淋漓尽致，诗意联想情节逼真。贵妃被诛杀之日，禁军杀了杨国忠之后仍驻马不前，提出杨妃不死不足以息众怒。回想起多年前七夕夜的海誓山盟，是多么悲伤啊！唐玄宗身为帝王连宠妃都保不住，真不如民间的普通夫妻呢！讽刺、叹息之意，油然而生。

On Lady Yang's Death

(II)

'Tis said there is a fairyland over the sea.
When this life is no more, can there another be?
In vain the watchman beat at night the warning gong;
No cock would wake her from dream with morning song.
The six armies demanded her death left and right.
Could she still laugh at severed lover-stars at night?
Though the emperor reigned as long as forty years,
She's not so happy as a griefless maid appears.

Note: Lady Yang was the favorite mistress of the Bright Emperor of the Tang Dynasty. When the six armies in revolt demanded her death, the emperor could not save her.

富平少侯[①]

① 富平少侯：西汉景帝时张安世被封为富平侯，他的孙子张放年少时即继承爵位，史称“富平少侯”。

七国[②]三边[③]未到忧，
十三身袭富平侯。
不收金弹抛林外，
却惜银床在井头。
彩树转灯珠错落，
绣檀回枕玉雕锼[④]。
当关[⑤]不报侵晨客[⑥]，
新得佳人字莫愁。

② 七国：汉景帝时的七个同姓诸侯国：吴、楚、赵、胶东、胶西、济南、淄川。他们曾联合发动叛乱。此处指藩镇割据叛乱。

③ 三边：战国时期燕赵秦与匈奴接壤，后来便以燕赵秦所在地为三边，即幽州、并州、凉州。此处指边患。

④ 玉雕锼：形容檀木枕刻镂精巧，像玉一样莹润精美。锼，刻镂。

⑤ 当关：守门人。

⑥ 侵晨客：清早来访的客人。

该诗塑造了一个荒淫奢侈、醉生梦死的贵族公子哥形象，他不知内忧外患，只顾挥霍浪费，荒淫好色，映射了当时晚唐危机四伏的社会环境，也暗示了让这种纨绔子弟身居高位，是政治腐败、国运不振的重要根源。

A Young Lord

Not worried about separatists nor frontiers,
He inherited his lordship at thirteen years.
He'd let his golden balls roll away left and right,
But love beside the well the windlass silver-bright.
His pillars decorated with lanterns pearls-made;
His sandalwood pillow seemed made of sculptured jade.
No early visitor would be announced by day,
For with his favorite griefless mistress he'd stay.

Note: It is said that this is a satire against the young emperor Jing Zong of the Tang Dynasty(唐敬宗).

离亭[①]赋得折杨柳[②]

（二首其一）

① 离亭：离别的驿站。

② 赋得折杨柳：赋诗来咏折柳送别。

暂凭樽酒送无憀[③]，
莫损愁眉与细腰。
人世死前唯有别，
春风争拟惜长条。

③ 无憀：即无聊，无所依赖，指愁苦。

这是一首讲惜别的诗。前两句和后两句一个谓之勿折杨柳，一个谓之不惜折杨柳，看似矛盾，其实各有深意，极尽表达了惜别之情。

Breaking Willow Twigs at Parting

(I)

What can I do but pour wine for your broken heart?
Don't aggravate your eyebrows and waist slender!
Before our death there's nothing sadder than to part,
Why should the vernal breeze save willow branches tender?

Note: The breaking of a twig from the willow tree was a symbol to show the grief at parting. So the poet urges his lover to break more so as to lessen her grief as if a greater grief might diminish a lesser one.

离亭赋得折杨柳

（二首其二）

含烟惹雾[1]每依依[2]，

万绪千条拂落晖。

为报行人休尽折，

半留相送半迎归。

① 含烟惹雾：笼罩在烟雾中的茂密的柳条。

② 依依：状恋恋不舍。

前半描写杨柳的风姿可爱，无论在烟雾之中，还是在夕阳之下，都是千枝万缕，依依有情。杨柳如此多情，既管送人，也管迎人，不必将它一齐折掉。折掉一半，送人；留下一半，迎人，岂不妙哉。该诗匠心独具，构思高超。

Breaking Willow Twigs at Parting

(II)

Willow leaves drink smoke and mist, unwilling to leave,
And thousands of branches caress the setting sun.
Don't break all the twigs. O' lover, lest it should grieve
Your friend on his return to see all trees stripped and done.

Note: The willow tree was not only a symbol of grief at parting but also a witness of joy at meeting or reunion.

宫妓

珠箔轻明拂玉墀[①]，
披香新殿斗腰支。
不须看尽鱼龙戏，
终遣君王怒偃师[②]。

① 玉墀：白玉台阶。

② 偃师：古代的巧匠。

本篇虽以“宫妓”为题，但其意并不在描述宫妓舞技斗艳或讥刺帝王荒淫无度的生活，而是针对内庭中诡计多端的阴谋权变者而发出的幽默讽刺。宫内的佞臣贼子如美人争风斗艳般争权博弈的举动无时不有，但尽管他们诡计多端、权谋尽展，终有一天将被识破，一定会自食其恶果。

Palace Dancers

The crystal screens caressed the royal steps of jade;
The dancers vied to show slender waist in brocade.
Although the fish and dragon play might please the Sire,
The musician risked to be killed at his ire.

Note: On the dancing ground caressed by crystal screens, dancers tried to play fish or dragon by showing their slender waist. But if their play aroused the king's anger, the musician would run the risk of being killed. This is a satire against the ruler.

宫 辞

君恩如水[1]向东流，
得宠忧移失宠愁。
莫向尊前[2]奏花落，
凉风只在殿西头。

① 君恩如水：君王的恩泽就像流水般漂移不定。

② 尊前：宴席上。

本篇与《宫妓》诗意相近，也可称之为姊妹篇，为讥讽牛党得宠者而作。一、二句是说君恩如日夜向东流淌的河水，谁也不可能把它留住。权力既能得之，也能失去，患得患失是这些人的通病。三、四句敬告受宠者不要得意忘形，应自当猛醒。

A Palace Poem

Imperial favor flows like eastward running stream;
When won, it brings tear for loss; when lost, it brings woe.
Don't sing before winecups the Fallen Blossom's Dream,
For from Western Palace the cold wind will soon blow.

Note: The last two lines might serve as a warning against those who have won the imperial favor.

代　赠

（二首其一）

楼上黄昏欲望休，
玉梯横绝[①]月中钩。
芭蕉不展丁香结，
同向春风各自愁。

① 玉梯横绝：华美的楼梯横断，无由得上。

该诗以一女子的口吻，写她不能与情人相会的愁绪，以芭蕉心之卷缩未伸和丁香花蕊刚刚初露尚未绽放来比喻双方的不解之愁和相思之苦，同时还含有两位缘分未到，天意不助之意，无限惆怅。

Lovesickness

(I)

At dusk she will not gaze afar in tower high;

The hook-like moon shines on untrodden stairs nearby.

Banana leaves uprolled and lilacs in knot

Reveal their lovesickness the vernal breeze knows not.

Note: Banana and lilacs waiting for the breeze are symbols of the lovesick waiting in vain for their lover.

楚　吟

山[1]上离宫[2]宫上楼，
楼前宫畔暮江流。
楚天长短[3]黄昏雨，
宋玉[4]无愁亦自愁。

① 山：指巫山。

② 离宫：巫山西北的楚宫。

③ 长短：无论长短。即“总之”，“横竖”。

④ 宋玉：战国楚辞赋家。

诗人乘舟行至江陵时欣然观景，见江畔上山峦起伏，巍然壮观，山上有离宫高楼耸立，遥想如在黄昏时从宫楼上俯视山下即可见江水奔流，大自然真是美不胜收。紧接着，诗人联想到自己的现实处境，心情压抑，精神不振，想起古人宋玉的苦衷，身世沉沦，仕宦坎坷，更何况在秋雨黄昏之时，自然触景伤情，悲凉无限。

The Southern King's Tryst with the Mountain Goddess

Uphill the palace stands, above the halls a bower,
The stream before the halls carries twilight away.
The evening sky brings flesh showers for thirsting flower.
How could the griefless poet without sorrow stay?

Note: The griefless poet in the last line refers to Song Yu（宋玉）who wrote about the dream of the Southern King's（楚襄王）tryst with the Goddess of Mount Witch（巫山神女）in the bower uphill.The poet is grieved for the king of the Tang Dynasty also dreams of his own joy without doing good to the people.

瑶　池

瑶池阿母绮窗开，
黄竹歌[1]声动地哀。
八骏[2]日行三万里，
穆王何事不重来。

①黄竹歌：逸诗，也作《黄竹诗》。借《黄竹》哀歌以寓穆王之崩。

②八骏：传说周穆王有八匹骏马，可日行三万里。

此诗以《穆天子传》所载的西王母与周穆王相约见面的传说来构思，讥刺了皇帝求仙的虚妄。晚唐迷信求长生不老之风尤为盛行，宪宗、穆宗、武宗等皆因四处求仙、服丹药妄求长生而丧命，诗人以此诗嘲讽那些统治者，恰如其分。

The Pond of Jewels

The Queen of Jewel Pond opened her window wide
But only heard grievous songs rolling to her side.
The royal steeds could run ten thousand miles a day
Why did the emperor not come again and stay?

Note: The Goddess of Jewel Pond waited in vain for the arrival of Emperor Zhou Mu（周穆王）whose steeds could run ten thousand miles a day. This verse shows that even a goddess could not immortalize an emperor.

韩冬郎①即席为诗相送（韩冬郎即席为诗相送，一座皆惊。他日余方追吟“连宵侍坐徘徊久”之句有老成之风，因成二绝寄酬，兼呈畏之员外）

（二首其一）

① 韩冬郎：韩偓，冬郎是其小名。

十岁②裁诗走马成③，
冷灰残烛动离情。
桐花④万里丹山⑤路，
雏凤清于老凤声。

② 十岁：大中五年（851年），韩偓十岁。

③ 走马成：言其作诗文思敏捷，走马之间即可成章。

④ 桐花：《诗经·大雅·卷阿》：“凤皇鸣矣，于彼高岗。梧桐生矣，于彼朝阳。”泛指后起之秀将更有作为，不可限量。桐，梧桐，传说凤凰非梧桐不宿。

⑤ 丹山：传说为凤凰产地。

韩偓之父韩瞻，与李商隐是同年进士，又是连襟，二人交谊很深，题中畏之员外即指韩瞻。唐宣宗大中五年（851年），李商隐赴梓州为节度书记。其时韩偓八岁，即席赋诗，才惊满座。该诗追忆了韩冬郎十岁即席赋诗的事，称赞他才思敏捷，所作诗歌富于情感，就连冷灰残烛也为之感动。第三、四句把韩冬郎比喻为凤凰，称赞其前程远大，如万里之遥的丹山碧梧之雏凤，其才华建树必胜老凤（韩瞻）。

Written for Han Wo, Poet Prodigy

(I)

You wrote a verse with highest speed at ten years old;
We would not part though candle ashes turned cold.
The flowery mountain path extends for miles long;
The young surpass the old in singing phoenix's song.

Note: Han Wo was son of Han Chan, son-in-law of Wang Maoyuan as the poet Li Shangyin. Li was invited by Han in 851 when Han Wo wrote a verse at ten years old in the farewell feast, and Li wrote the above in 855 in reply when he returned to the capital.

板桥[1]晓别

① 板桥：指开封城西的板桥。

回望高城落晓河[2]，
长亭窗户压微波[3]。
水仙欲上鲤鱼[4]去，
一夜芙蓉红泪[5]多。

② 晓河：指银河。

③ 微波：指银河之波，也指长亭下水渠之波。

④ 鲤鱼：典故出自《列仙传》，一名赵国人琴高，会神仙术，曾乘赤鲤来，留月余复入水去。

⑤ 红泪：《拾遗记》记录，魏文帝美人薛灵芸离别父母登车上路，用王唾壶承泪，壶呈红色，及至京师，壶中泪凝如血。

这是一首送别之作，情深而不俗气，典雅而意味绵长，且十分富有想象力。

Parting at Morning on the Wooden Bridge

The Milky Way fades over the high city wall;
The parting pavilion overlooks the rippling stream.
The fairy riding a carp goes up the waterfall,
Leaving the lotus bloom shed red tears in her dream.

Note: The poet describes the parting of two lovers at dawn, comparing the one who leaves to a fairy and the other who stays to a lotus flower.

银河吹笙

怅望银河吹玉笙[1]，

楼寒院冷接平明。

重衾[2]幽梦[3]他年断，

别树[4]羁雌[5]昨夜惊。

月榭故香因雨发，

风帘残烛隔霜清。

不须浪作缑山意[6]，

湘瑟[7]秦箫自有情。

① 玉笙：笙之美称。

② 重衾：两层衾被，借以喻男女欢会。

③ 幽梦：隐约不明之梦境。

④ 别树：树的斜枝。

⑤ 羁雌：失偶之雌鸟。

⑥ 缑山意：指入道修仙。缑山，即缑氏山，在今河南省偃师市东南。刘向《列仙传·王子乔》："王子乔者，周灵王太子晋，好吹笙，道士浮丘公接以上嵩山成仙。三十余年后，乘白鹤于山头，举手谢时人，数日乃去。"李白《凤笙篇》："绿云紫气向函关，访道应寻缑氏山。"

⑦ 湘瑟：湘灵鼓瑟，即湘水女神鼓瑟传情。

本诗打破了时间与空间的顺序和逻辑联系，跳跃性极强，但也显得晦涩难懂。首联写吹笙的环境；颔联写吹笙的内容；联写眼前景物，虚实结合，情景交融；尾联抒发诗人的梦想与执着。构思实在巧妙。

Playing on Flute in Sight of the Silver River

Gazing on Milky Way, on flute of jade I play
In bower and courtyard cold near the break of day.
Gone are sweet dreams in heavy quilt of bygone year;
A lonely bird on lonely tree shivers with fear.
Fragrance of moonlit bower spreads out with the rain;
Flickering candle flame and frost sing the retrain.
Why should you go on crane divine to Heaven high?
The music played by fairies would bring you to the sky.

Note: The last line says in conclusion that the music played by fairies would bring a lonely heart to the sky as a crane divine does.

夕阳楼[1]

[1] 夕阳楼：旧郑州之名胜，始建于北魏，为中国唐宋八大名楼之一，曾与黄鹤楼、鹳雀楼、岳阳楼等齐名。

花明柳暗绕天愁，
上尽重城[2]更上楼。
欲问孤鸿向何处，
不知身世自悠悠。

[2] 重城：即“层楼”，指高高的城楼。

李商隐以夕阳楼为题作此诗，寓意是以物思人，表达他对曾经帮助引荐过他的萧澥遭贬的同情之心，抒发自己的怀念和愁苦抑郁的心情。“孤鸿”能飞向何处呢？又联想想起自己不也是处处皆为客，生计毫无着落，长时间漂泊四方吗？

The Sunset Tower

Flowers and willows exhale sorrow to the sky,
I mount the tower higher and higher stage by stage.
I try to ask the lonely swan where he will fly.
Forgetting my own loneliness is in lonely age.

春 雨

帐卧新春白袷衣①，
白门②寥落意多违。
红楼③隔雨相望冷，
珠箔飘灯独自归。
远路应悲春晼晚④，
残宵犹得梦依稀。
玉珰⑤缄札⑥何由达，
万里云罗一雁飞。

① 白袷衣：即白夹衣，唐人以白衫为闲居便服。

② 白门：金陵的别称，即现江苏省南京市。

③ 红楼：华美的楼房，多指女子的住处。

④ 晼晚：夕阳西下的光景。

⑤ 玉珰：是用玉做的耳坠，古代常用环佩、玉珰一类的饰物作为男女定情的信物。

⑥ 缄札：指书信。

诗人旧地重游，恰逢绵绵春雨飘洒，天空中阴云笼罩。题虽然作“春雨”，却并非直接写春雨，而是抒写在春夜雨中的相思之情。

Spring Rain

Gloomy in early spring, I lie still clad in white;
How much I miss our rendezvous now in sad plight!
Your rosy bower chills my heart when viewed in rain;
Back when dim lamplight is screened, lonely I remain.
Far on your way, you should be grieved when spring is late;
Deep in the night, I but dimly dream of my mate.
How could I send my love letter with two jade rings?
Could miles of clouds be pierced by a swan on the wings?

楚宫

湘波如泪色漻漻[1]，
楚厉[2]迷魂逐恨遥。
枫树夜猿愁自断，
女萝[3]山鬼[4]语相邀。
空归腐败犹难复，
更困腥臊岂易招。
但使故乡三户[5]在，
彩丝[6]谁惜惧长蛟。

① 漻漻：水清澈状。

② 楚厉：指屈原。屈原投江而死，无后人、无归处，古称“鬼无所归则为厉”。

③ 女萝：菟丝，一种缘物而生的藤蔓。

④ 山鬼：山中之神，因为非正神，故称“鬼”。

⑤ 三户：指楚人。《史记·项羽本纪》：“楚虽三户，亡秦必楚。”

⑥ 彩丝：指五彩丝线扎成的粽子。

本篇是为凭吊屈原而作，但并未从屈原的人品才能和政治上的不幸遭遇着笔，通篇都在写屈原的“迷魂”，景象凄迷，悲情如海，让人含恨无穷。

To the Poet Drowned in the Southern Lake

The waves of the Southern Lake roll with bitter tears,
Your enchanted soul goes with the waves far away.
The ape on maple tree wails and then disappears.
The mountain fairy in ivy leaves would show you the way.
Your putrid body could not come to life again.
How could your soul get rid of the fishes' stinking smell?
But so long as your younger Southerners remain,
Their long long rope would bind the long long serpent fell.

Note: The poet, a loyal minister banished by the king of Chu（楚王）drowned himself in the Southern Lake 2000 years ago.

晚　晴

深居俯夹城①，
春去夏犹清。
天意怜幽草，
人间重晚晴。
并添高阁迥，
微注②小窗明。
越鸟③巢干后，
归飞体更轻。

① 夹城：城门外的曲城。

② 微注：晚景斜晖，光线显得微弱和柔和，故说"微注"。

③ 越鸟：南方的鸟。

本诗通过夹城雨后见霁阳的观感，抒发诗人愉悦的心情。笔触明快，感情细腻。特别是颔联"天意怜幽草，人间重晚晴"一句更是意境深远，耐人寻味，被世代传诵。

A Sunny Evening after Rain

I look down on town wall from my retreat;
With spring just gone, summer weather is clear.
It's Heaven's will to pity green grass sweet;
In human world sunny evening's held dear.
I can see afar from my tower high;
The parting rays make my small window bright.
The Southern birds find their nest again dry;
When they fly back, they feel their bodies light.

安定[1]城楼

① 安定：郡名，即泾州，今甘肃省平凉市泾川县北，唐代泾原节度使的治所。

迢递[2]高城百尺楼，
绿杨枝外尽汀洲。
贾生[3]年少虚垂泪，
王粲[4]春来更远游。
永忆江湖归白发，
欲回天地入扁舟。
不知腐鼠成滋味，
猜意鹓雏[5]竟未休。

② 迢递：此形容楼高而且连续绵延。

③ 贾生：贾谊（前200年—前168年），西汉初年著名政论家、文学家，世称贾生。

④ 王粲：东汉末年人，建安七子之一。年轻时曾流寓荆州，依附刘表，但并不得志。

⑤ 鹓雏：古代传说中一种像凤凰的鸟。

春风吹柳的季节，诗人登上泾源古城头——安定城楼，纵目远眺，看到朝政的混乱，腐败势力的横行，有理想和才干的人无从施展自己的抱负，心中不禁生起了哀国忧时和自伤身世的无穷感触。此诗意境深远，充分表达了诗人的博大胸怀，备受后人推崇。尤其“永忆江湖归白发，欲回天地入扁舟”一句，使后人颇为赞赏，常诵常新，回味无穷。

On the Tower of the City Wall

From hundred-foot-high city wall I look afar;
Beyond green willow branches sandy islets are.
I remember a student while young shed vain tears,
And a famed scholar roamed in the spring of his years.
I can't forget white-haired General on the lake floating
After changing the face of the world he went boating.
An owl might feed on dead rats with good appetite,
But a phoenix would perch on trees of lofty height.

Note: The poet compares himself with two unsuccessful scholars, regrets his failure to realize his ideal like the general and shows his disdain for those who seek fortune and fame.

天涯

春日在天涯[①]，

天涯日又斜。

莺啼如有泪，

为湿最高花[②]。

① 天涯：此处泛指家乡以外的极远之地。

② 最高花：树梢顶上的花。

春天到了，但诗人并没有感到春机盎然和充满希望的美景，只觉得春日遥远，表现了诗人孤寂和悲愁的心境。

The End of the Sky

Spring is far, far away
Where the sun slants its ray.
If orioles have tear,
Wet highest flowers here!

Note: This quatrain may be said to be an elegy of spring, of the poet's life and of his era. The place is far away and the time is late, even a happy bird would be saddened to shed tears on beautiful flowers.

日 日

日日春光斗日光，
山城斜路杏花香。
几时心绪浑无事，
得及游丝[①]百尺长。

①游丝：指春天时虫类吐在空中而四处飞扬的细丝。

这是一首描绘春天的诗，自然之景与诗人的心绪似乎有着千丝万缕的关系。

From Day to Day

From day to day in splendor spring with sunlight vies,
The sloping hillside way sweet with apricot bloom.
When could my heart-string be as free from worldly ties
As the hundred-foot-long gossamer in the gloom?

Note: The poet asks why men and things should vie in splendor and flagrance, and whether it is worthwhile or not to be flee as the gossamer.

龙 池

龙池[①]赐酒敞云屏，
羯鼓[②]声高众乐停。
夜半宴归宫漏永[③]，
薛王[④]沉醉寿王[⑤]醒。

① 龙池：既是地名，也是舞曲名。这里指皇帝的宫殿。

② 羯鼓：一种出自外夷的乐器，据说来源于羯族。

③ 漏永：形容漫漫长夜。漏，古代的计时器。

④ 薛王：唐玄宗弟弟李业之子。

⑤ 寿王：唐玄宗的儿子李瑁。

这是一首咏史诗，表达了作者对封建帝王骄奢淫逸的不满和嘲讽。

Dragon Pool Feast

At Dragon Pool feast spread screens embroidered with cloud,
All music drowned in the emperor's drumbeats loud.
Come back at midnight to hear the waterclock's song,
The prince not drunken lay awake all the night long.

Note: Lady Yang(杨贵妃), former wife of the prince(寿王)became the emperor's(唐玄宗) favorite concubine, so the prince could not fall asleep after the emperor's feast.

流莺[1]

①流莺：漂荡流转的黄莺。

流莺漂荡复参差，
渡陌临流不自持。
巧啭岂能无本意，
良辰未必有佳期。
风朝露夜阴晴里，
万户千门开闭时。
曾苦伤春不忍听，
凤城[2]何处有花枝[3]。

②凤城：借指京城长安。

③花枝：指流莺的栖息之所。

这首诗描写了流莺无所依托的漂泊感，凄凉婉转，细腻幽微。流莺的巧啭声，似乎也是作者的心声。

To the Roving Oriole

Oriole roving high and low,
Are you happy over fields and streams?
What does your warbling want to show?
Can the fine days fulfil your dreams?
You are careless of shine or rain,
Dawn or dusk, open or closed door.
I'm grieved to hear your sad refrain.
When spring is gone and blooms no more.

Note: The poet is grieved to hear the roving oriole whose warbling reminds him of his unfulfilled dream.

七月二十九日崇让宅[1]宴作

①崇让宅：诗人的岳父、泾原节度使王茂元在东都洛阳崇让坊的宅邸，诗人和妻子曾在此居住。

露如微霰[2]下前池，
月过回塘万竹悲。
浮世本来多聚散，
红蕖[3]何事亦离披。
悠扬归梦惟灯见，
濩落生涯独酒知。
岂到白头长只尔，
嵩阳松雪有心期。

②微霰：微细的雪粒。

③红蕖：红荷花。蕖，芙蕖。

此诗的前半写初秋崇让宅的景象，崇让宅因长时间无人居住，已经变成了废宅，寂无一人，无比悲凉；后半诗人直抒胸臆，表现出一种冷落、孤寂之感。

Written at a Family Feast on the 29th Day of the 7th Moon

The poolside dew congealed into frost before the door.
The wind sweeps by and the bamboo shivers all the more.
It's nothing strange for people to meet and to part.
Why should the lotus blooms waver and grieve my heart?
Only my lamplight sees the homesickness of mine,
My dreary life can't be consoled by a cup of wine.
Shall I remain so until all my hair grows white?
A mountain rich in pines and snow would be my site.

吴　宫[1]

① 吴宫：春秋末年吴王夫差所建宫殿。

龙槛[2]沉沉水殿清，
禁门[3]深掩断人声。
吴王宴罢满宫醉，
日暮水漂花出城。

② 龙槛：宫中临水有栏杆的亭轩类建筑。
③ 禁门：宫禁的大门。

该诗借咏史以讽刺封建王侯的荒奢，王公贵族们成天沉迷于醉生梦死的奢靡生活中，老百姓却民不聊生，过着食不果腹、饥寒交迫的生活。诗人借古慨今，用心良苦，色彩鲜明，言尽而味无穷。

The Eastern Palace

Shadows of poolside bowers cast on water clear,
All the doors closed, merry-making noises disappear.
After the royal feast all the palace is drank.
Only fallen petals flow out when the sun is sunk.

嫦　娥

云母屏风[1]烛影深，

长河渐落晓星沉。

嫦娥应悔偷灵药，

碧海青天夜夜心[2]。

①云母屏风：以云母石制作的屏风。

②夜夜心：指嫦娥每晚都会感到孤单。

此诗咏叹嫦娥在月中的孤寂情景，猜想嫦娥后悔偷了后羿的药奔月，结果只能独居清冷的月宫中，孤独后悔，抒发诗人自伤之情。

To the Moon Goddess

Upon the marble screen the candlelight is winking;
The Silver River slants and morning stars are sinking.
You'd regret to have stolen the miraculous potion;
Each night you brood over the lonely celestial ocean.

Note: The Moon Goddess was said to have been the wife of the miraculous Archer who had shot down nine suns from the sky and was awarded with the elixir, but his wife stole it, ate it, flew to the moon and became the solitary Moon Goddess. The poet writes this verse to show himself as solitary as the Moon Goddess brooding over the lonely sky.

忆住一师[①]

① 住一师：僧人，诗人的好友。

无事经年别远公[②]，
帝城[③]钟晓[④]忆西峰[⑤]。
炉烟消尽寒灯晦，
童子开门雪满松。

② 远公：东晋庐山东林寺高僧惠远，是净土宗的初祖。诗人以净土宗的初祖慧远大师借指住一。

③ 帝城：指京城长安。

④ 钟晓：即晓钟，是唐代京城长安清晨的一大特色，每天拂晓，宫中和各佛寺的钟一齐长鸣，声震全城。

⑤ 西峰：指庐山。

每天拂晓，京城长安的宫中和各佛寺的钟声一齐长鸣，声震全城，自然使诗人联想到西峰的住一师，想起了这位相别多年的有人。后两句，诗人重现了一个场景：住一师处于居室，不觉烟炉中焚香将尽，寒灯也渐暗；小童推开出门，只见皑皑白雪，洒满苍翠的松枝。清晨的钟声，把诗人带到当年与住一师同在西峰时的情景中，饱含着诗人队友人深沉的忆念之情。

For the Priest of Western Peak

Why should I leave the priest of Western Peak for years?
Even the royal morning bell spreads to the west.
The incense burned up, dim his lantern light appears,
His door is opened to pine and snow on the crest.

微　雨

初随林霭[1]动，
稍共夜凉分。
窗迥侵灯冷，
庭虚[2]近水闻。

①林霭：林中的云气。

②虚：这里是空旷的意思。

李商隐的咏物诗，摹写入微，细致传神。云气弥漫，夜晚微凉，空寂的庭院里，轻响着细微的淅沥声，别有意境。

A Slight Rain

You seem to see a floating vapor rise
And feel the coolness of night vaporize.
Through open window it flickers lamplight,
An empty poolside hall hears it alight.

细　雨

帷飘白玉堂，
簟[①]卷碧牙床。
楚女[②]当时意，
萧萧[③]发彩[④]凉。

① 簟：竹席。
② 楚女：指《楚辞》里描写的神女。
③ 萧萧：凉意。
④ 发彩：发光可鉴。

白玉堂，指天宫，碧牙床，指天空，细雨由天上洒落，有如天宫白玉堂前飘拂下垂的帷幕，又像是从天空这张碧牙床上翻卷下来的簟席。该诗极富想象力。

A Fine Rain

Screen wafting before the hall of white jade,
Mat rolled down from bed of ivory made.
Hair falling down of a fair Southern Flower,
Coolness of breath exhaled shower by shower.

Note: A fine rain is compared to a wafting screen, a mat rolled down from bed, hair falling on fair shoulders or cool breath exhaled by a beauty.

无　题

（二首其一）

凤尾香罗[①]薄几重，
碧文圆顶夜深缝。
扇裁月魄羞难掩，
车走雷声语未通。
曾是寂寥金烬暗，
断无消息石榴红[②]。
斑骓只系垂杨岸，
何处西南任好风。

①凤尾香罗：织有彩凤图纹的芳香的罗帐。

②石榴红：指石榴花开的季节。

诗人深夜难眠，回忆起当时与情人偶遇的情景。春光已逝，石榴花开，相思之人却杳无音信，令人苦闷感伤。

Untitled

(I)

On manifold silk canopy with phoenix tail
She stitches green patterns in the deep of night.
Shy looked her face the moon-shaped fan could hardly veil;
Gone was his rolling cab, speechless, soon lost to sight.
The lonely candle sheds its dim light to deplore;
Red pomegranates see her wait for news with zest.
His dappled horse is tethered to the willow shore.
When can she enjoy the good wind from southwest?

Note: This poem describes the lovesickness of the lonely heroine stitching patterns on the silk canopy for her lover who passed by her in a rolling cab and tethered his horse to the willow tree without giving her further news from the southwest.

无　题

（二首其二）

重帏深下莫愁堂，
卧后清宵细细长。
神女[①]生涯原是梦，
小姑[②]居处本无郎。
风波不信菱枝弱，
月露谁教桂叶香。
直道相思了无益，
未妨惆怅是清狂。

①神女：宋玉《神女赋》中的巫山神女。

②小姑：古乐府《青溪小姑曲》：“小姑所居，独处无郎。”

这首诗描写男女之情，却又道出了相思无益之言，全诗意境深远，措辞委婉，具有较高的艺术价值。

Untitled

(II)

The grief laden curtains hang deep in her Griefless Hall,
Awake from sleeps, she finds the sleepless night grow long.
A happy life in love is a dream beyond call;
A lonely virgin deprived of amorous song.
Against the wind and waves can't stand her cresses frail.
Will the moon shed dew to make her laurel leaves sweet?
Although she knows her lovesickness of no avail,
How can a passionate poor heart no longer beat?

Note: This poem describes the sleepless night of a solitary woman in her Griefless Hall.

贾　生[1]

① 贾生：贾谊(前200年—前168年)，西汉初年著名政论家、文学家，世称贾生。贾谊少有才名，文帝时任博士，迁太中大夫，受大臣周勃、灌婴排挤，谪为长沙王太傅，故后世亦称贾长沙、贾太傅。三年后被召回长安，为梁怀王太傅。梁怀王坠马而死，贾谊深自歉疚，抑郁而亡，时仅三十三岁。

宣室[2]求贤访逐臣[3]，
贾生才调更无伦。
可怜夜半虚前席，
不问苍生问鬼神。

② 宣室：汉代长安城中未央宫前殿的正室。

③ 逐臣：被放逐之臣，指贾谊曾被贬谪。

贾生即贾谊，西汉著名的文学家。年少时就才名远扬。一方面，诗人仿佛是在颂扬文帝虚怀若谷、求贤若渴，在听取贤才建议时态度诚恳；另一方面，读者似乎身临其境，感受到了贾谊口若悬河、侃侃而谈、才气四溢的场景。同时，借贾谊的遭遇，诗人书写了自己怀才不遇的感慨。

A Bright Scholar

The emperor recalled the banished scholar bright,
Peerless in eloquence and in ability.
Alas! His Majesty drew near him at midnight
To consult not on man but on divinity.

Note: The poet compares himself with the bright scholar whom the Han emperor consulted on divinity and not on state affairs, while he himself is not consulted at all.

谒[1] 山

① 谒：拜见。

从来系日乏长绳[2]，
水去云回恨不胜。
欲就麻姑[3]买沧海，
一杯春露冷如冰。

② 系日乏长绳：傅玄《九曲歌》中有“岁暮景迈群光绝，安得长绳系白日”，指时光难以留住。

③ 麻姑：传说中的女仙。

自古以来，就没有能够拴住太阳的长绳，时间的流逝无法阻止，逝川东去、白云归山，诗人在感叹时光易逝。如果麻姑能够将沧海买下，时光是不是就会走得慢一些？然而，一切皆是泡影，只剩下一杯冰冷的春露，令人不胜怅惘。该诗新奇浪漫，富于诗情，耐人寻味。

On the Mountain

Since olden days there is no rope to bind the sun.
How could we stop the cloud and water on the run?
I'd like to buy the vast sea from the goddess nice,
But a cup of spring dew soon turns as cold as ice.

Note: The poet standing at the top of a mountain regrets he could not stop the running of the sun, of floating clouds and flowing water.

哭刘司户蕡

路有论冤谪，
言皆在中兴。
空闻迁贾谊①，
不待相孙弘②。
江阔惟回首，
天高但抚膺③。
去年相送地，
春雪满黄陵。

①贾谊：（前200年—前168年），西汉初年著名政论家、文学家，世称贾生。贾谊少有才名，文帝时任博士，迁太中大夫，受大臣周勃、灌婴排挤，谪为长沙王太傅，故后世亦称贾长沙、贾太傅。三年后被召回长安，为梁怀王太傅。梁怀王坠马而死，贾谊深自歉疚，抑郁而亡，时仅三十三岁。

②孙弘：公孙弘，汉武帝时初为博士，一度免归，后又受到重用，官至丞相，封平津侯。

③抚膺：抚摩或捶拍胸口。表示惋惜、哀叹、悲愤等。

刘蕡冤谪而死，诗人借路人之口谈论冤谪，不仅表现了对刘蕡的同情和敬重，也从侧面反映了对宦官诬陷刘蕡的痛恨和谴责。

Elegy on Liu Fen

Caring but for prosperity,
You were degraded unjustly
Like the banished scholar-sage
Not to be promoted to peerage.
Turning to see the River wide,
I beat my breast and deeply sighed.
Now where last year we bade goodbye.
Snow's whitened yellow mountains high.

凉　思

客去波平槛，
蝉休露满枝。
永怀当此节，
倚立自移时。
北斗①兼春远，
南陵②寓使③迟。
天涯占梦数，
疑误有新知④。

①北斗：即北斗星。

②南陵：今安徽省芜湖市南陵县，唐时属宣州。

③寓使：传书的使者。寓，寄，托。

④新知：新结交的知己。

秋天到来，天气渐凉，诗人回忆起友人的离去，无比思念。该诗用词简练，情深意长。

Autumn Thoughts

Guests gone, waves level with the balustrade,
Cicadas silent, branches wet with dew.
How can I forget what is done and made
Standing there for hours, I'm thinking of you.
Two years stand between me and Northern Star.
No news from Southern home, it's overdue.
I can but dream and divine from afar,
Doubting if you have made connaissance new.

Note: The Northern Star refers to the capital.

花下醉

寻芳不觉醉流霞[1]，
倚树沉眠[2]日已斜。
客散酒醒深夜后，
更持红烛赏残花。

①流霞：神话传说中一种仙酒。《论衡·道虚》上说，项曼卿好道学仙，离家三年而返，自言："欲饮食，仙人辄饮我以流霞。每饮一杯，数日不饥。"此处是将似锦的繁花比作漫天的流霞之意。

②沉眠：醉酒之后的深睡。

诗人对花陶醉流连，因为爱花，所以怀着浓厚的兴致去"寻芳"，竟不知不觉地"醉"了。直到日斜夜深，客人已经散去，酒也已经醒了，四周是一片夜的朦胧与沉寂。夜色中，诗人持烛赏残花，别有一番滋味。

Intoxicated with Flowers

Drinking with rainbow cloud and flowers blooming bright,
Under a tree I fall asleep till sunset looms.
Guests gone, and sobered from wine in the deep of night,
Candle in hand, I go to see the overbloom.

正月崇让宅

密锁重关掩绿苔，
廊深阁迥此徘徊。
先知风起月含晕，
尚自露寒花未开。
蝙拂帘旌[①]终展转，
鼠翻窗网小惊猜。
背灯独共馀香语，
不觉犹歌起夜来[②]。

① 帘旌：帘箔，布门帘，因形似旌旗，故称。

②《起夜来》：乐府曲调名，《乐府解题》中说："《起夜来》，其辞意犹念畴昔思君之来也。"是妻子思念丈夫之辞。

这是诗人悼念亡妻之作，崇让宅是诗人的岳父、泾原节度使王茂元在东都洛阳崇让坊的宅邸，诗人和妻子曾在此居住。此次归来，昔人已不在，重门紧缩，庭院深深，只剩一片凄凉。全诗从白天到夜晚，由门外到宅内，通过这样的描写，衬托出诗人悼念妻子的悲痛心情和复杂的内心活动，不觉让人悲从中来。

Our Old Abode-Elegy on My Deceased Wife

Doors locked, curtain drawn down, mossy is our ground,
On winding corridor alone I would stroll around.
By lunar halo the rising wind is foretold.
How can the flowers bloom when drenched in dew cold?
I toss in bed when curtain's hit by a bat;
I am surprised to hear in the net squeak a rat.
Alone I talk with your shadow by the lamplight.
How can I help singing with you "Rising at Night"?

Note: The poet describes his dreary old abode after his wife's death.

骄儿诗

衮师①我骄儿，美秀乃无匹。
文葆②未周晬，固已知六七。
四岁知名姓，眼不视梨栗。
交朋颇窥观，谓是丹穴物③。
前朝尚器貌，流品方第一。
不然神仙姿，不尔燕鹤骨。
安得此相谓，欲慰衰朽质。
青春妍和月④，朋戏浑甥侄。
绕堂复穿林，沸若金鼎溢。

① 衮师：作者的儿子的名字。大约生于会昌六年（846年），此时约四岁。

② 文葆：包裹婴儿绣花小被。

③ 丹穴物：指凤凰。这里比喻衮师。

④ 妍和月：温暖的季节。

该诗是作者为自己的儿子李衮师所写，诗中描绘出一个天真活泼、聪明灵巧的儿童形象，与作者“憔悴欲四十，无肉畏蚤虱”形成鲜明对比，从而加深了对自己身世沉沦的感慨。全诗主要用叙事笔法，细节描写生动有趣。

Song of My Proud Son

I am proud of my son,
He is second to none.
Come down one year from Heaven,
He could tell six from seven.
Knowing his name at four,
No peers would he adore.
My friends would come and say
He is no common clay.
His appearance admired
Leaves nothing to be desired.
An immortal would fain
Say he's swallow or crane.
What my friends say, all told,
Would comfort a man old,
In vernal night or day
With his cousins he'd play.
They pass from hall to hall.
Boisterous one and all.

门有长者来，造次[①]请先出。

客前问所须，含意下吐实。

归来学客面，闱败秉爷笏。

或谑张飞胡，或笑邓艾吃。

豪鹰毛崱屴[②]，猛马气佶傈[③]。

截得青筼筜[④]，骑走恣唐突。

忽复学参军，按声唤苍鹘[⑤]。

又复纱灯旁，稽首[⑥]礼夜佛。

仰鞭罥[⑦]蛛网，俯首饮花蜜。

① 造次：匆忙间不顾礼节。

② 崱屴：高耸。

③ 佶傈：健壮。

④ 筼筜：竹子。

⑤ 参军、苍鹘：唐代参军戏中的主角和配角。

⑥ 稽首：叩拜。

⑦ 罥：挂。

When guests come to see me,
He would come out with glee.
When asked what he need,
He'd veil the truth, indeed,
He mimics one guest's face
In haste and without grace,
Another bearded guest
Stammering without rest.
Like an eagle in flight
Or a strong steed in fight.
He rides a hobby horse
Running with all its force.
He jeers at officers
Blaming their messengers.
By lamplight he makes vows
And to Buddha he bows.
He sweeps webs with his whip
And honey he would sip.

欲争蛱蝶轻，未谢柳絮疾。
阶前逢阿姊，六甲[1]颇输失。
凝走弄香奁，拔脱金屈戌。
抱持多反侧，威怒不可律。
曲躬牵窗网，衉唾拭琴漆。
有时看临书，挺立不动膝。
古锦请裁衣，玉轴亦欲乞。
请爷书春胜，春胜宜春日。
芭蕉斜卷笺，辛夷低过笔。

①六甲：一种棋类游戏。

As light as butterflies.

With willow down he vies.

Meeting his sister dear,

He plays game without fear.

He takes her toilet box

And breaks the golden locks.

Lying on ground, he'd stay;

Threatened, he'd not obey.

He draws the window screen,

Spits and wipes the lute clean.

Sometimes watching me write,

He stands unmoved, upright.

Of brocade he makes cover,

Of books he seems a lover.

Asking me to write "spring",

Of spring day he would sing.

Banana is paper white

Its bud a brush to write.

爷昔好读书，恳苦自著述。
憔悴欲四十，无肉畏蚤虱。
儿慎勿学爷，读书求甲乙[1]。
穰苴司马法[2]，张良黄石术。
便为帝王师，不假更纤悉。
况今西与北，羌戎正狂悖。
诛赦两未成，将养如痼疾。
儿当速成大，探雏入虎穴。
当为万户侯，勿守一经帙[3]。

① 甲乙：唐朝科举制度，录取进士分为甲、乙两第。

② 穰苴司马法：穰苴是春秋时齐国的名将，喜欢研究兵法。因曾任大司马而被称为“司马穰苴”。齐威王命人整理古代司马兵法，把穰苴兵法也附在其中，称为司马穰苴兵法，简称司马法（参《史记·司马穰苴列传》）。

③ 一经帙：经即儒家的经典。帙，书衣。

Then I was fond of books,
Studying long in my nooks.
At forty lean and wise.
I fear nor bug nor lice.
Do not learn to win fame
Like me without a name.
Try to learn from the sages
Of the different ages!
You'd be master of kings.
Carefree from trifling things.
The foe in the northwest
Are producing unrest.
Nor war nor peace can cure;
They're hard disease, for sure.
Grow up, be man of men,
Kill the foe in the den!
Son, be a hero brave
And not a scholar grave!

Note: The poet describes in detail the son he is proud of and lays his hope on.

图书在版编目（CIP）数据

许渊冲译李商隐诗选：汉文、英文 /（唐）李商隐著；许渊冲编译．-- 北京：中译出版社，2021.1（2022.6 重印）

ISBN 978-7-5001-6455-5

Ⅰ. ①许… Ⅱ. ①李… ②许… Ⅲ. ①唐诗－诗集－汉、英 Ⅳ. ①I222.742

中国版本图书馆 CIP 数据核字（2020）第 242942 号

出版发行 中译出版社
地　　址 北京市西城区新街口外大街28号普天德胜大厦主楼4层
电　　话 (010) 68359719
邮　　编 100088
电子邮箱 book@ctph.com.cn
网　　址 http://www.ctph.com.cn

出 版 人 乔卫兵
总 策 划 刘永淳
责任编辑 刘香玲　张　旭
文字编辑 王秋璎　张莞嘉　赵浠彤
营销编辑 毕竟方

封面制作 刘　哲
内文制作 黄　浩　北京竹页文化传媒有限公司
印　　刷 山东临沂新华印刷物流集团有限责任公司
经　　销 新华书店

规　　格 840mm×1092mm　1/32
印　　张 5.75
字　　数 160千
版　　次 2021年1月第1版
印　　次 2022年6月第3次

ISBN 978-7-5001-6455-5　定价：39.00元